I0556068

The Boxes

A novel by

Dr. Bonnie Benefield

THE BOXES

This book is a work of fiction. The names of characters, places and events arose from the author's imagination and are wholly fictitious. Any resemblance to places or persons, living or dead, is entirely coincidental.

Book cover graphics by Renee Luke of Cover Me Book Covers

ISBN 978-1-7325981-3-3

THE BOXES

Acknowledgments

This book is affectionately dedicated to my my sons Brandon and Brett Boeke for their love and support during the writing of this book. I also wish to thank my good friends Tami Overbury, Ron Feldman, and Maria Luongo for their help along with Renee Luke for the graphics on the book cover.

THE BOXES

DEDICATION

I wish to dedicate this book to my wonderful sons, Brandon and Brett Boeke who always encouraged me.

THE BOXES

Sal was sitting on the back deck of his boat enjoying the breeze and the gentle rocking from the waves. The only visible lights were from the cabin and the faint lights from the shore. His mind returned to Alexandra in quiet times like this, remembering how she laughed and filled a void in his life he never realized until she was gone. His yacht seemed lifeless without her despite the female companions he tried unsuccessfully to replace her. When they were together they never talked about love but he did love her. He hid his sadness and regret well.

His constant companions and bodyguards were in the cabin watching TV although they occasionally came out to check on him. Sal tried not to think of the many decisions he had to make. He was the head of the largest family for miles around and was responsible for resolving the disputes between all of the families regarding the vast businesses with which they were involved. Despite the very lucrative interests that they shared to varying degrees, there were often disagreements about the control and distribution of the proceeds. It was difficult to placate those that were dissatisfied with their share as they had strong opinions about what they expected. This conglomerate of Italian families had a lot of influence on law enforcement and politicians. Their influence was the result of large donations and gifts or favors that were granted which were not always legal.

Sal was a handsome man with even features and a full head of hair that was gray at his temples which made him look distinguished. He was muscular from regular exercise and well over six feet tall, although shorter than his large companions. He looked younger than his age of sixty. His bodyguards were carefully selected for their loyalty and ability to provide him protection.

Sal was occupied by his thoughts and he did not hear the sounds of the two figures clad in wet suits when they climbed onto the boat on other side of the deck. They were careful to leave their fins and oxygen tanks tied to the anchor chain. One man opened a vial of the choral hydrate he was carrying and poured the contents onto a cloth while taking care not to inhale the fumes. They soundlessly crept up behind Sal and pulled him off of the chair. While two men held him down the third one put his hand with the saturated cloth over Sal's mouth just long enough to subdue him. The chair was placed on its side by the railing to make it look as though Sal had just fallen overboard. The men inside the cabin did not hear what transpired on the deck. The wetsuit clad men were skilled to work quickly and dragged him to the other side of the deck where they soundlessly slipped him into the water. They quickly put on their gear and swam away believing he would drown and his body would wash up on a distant beach. They knew that any remnants of the drug used would be dispelled by the heartless water.

The assassins were too far away to notice that Sal had surfaced and had been revived enough by the cold water to enable him to throw his arm over the anchor chain. He was awake enough to wait until he was certain his assassins had fled. There were too many people who would want him dead and if they found out he was still alive, there would be another attempt on his life. Retaliation would be too difficult without knowing who scheduled his demise. His life was in danger. Sal wondered if his allegedly loyal bodyguards were involved in this attempt on his life. His curiosity turned to anger especially since Sal had been generous to his bodyguards taking care of them in addition to their salaries. He now distrusted everyone and he knew that a large sum of money can corrupt anyone. He knew what he had to do.

An hour later, Sal's employees went to the deck looking for him and found his shoes and the deck chair leaning against the railing. The men did not find him after an extensive search of the boat and now believed that he was lost overboard. Their lack of emotion was telling. During their search they failed to notice that there was a small dingy missing from the boat.

THE BOXES

CHAPTER 1

DINNER

The evening was cool with a mild mist, and fortunately the heavy rain had stopped leaving only a light drizzle. Alexandra, although everyone called her Alex, was pleased that the heavy downpour had ceased as she never remembered or bothered to bring her umbrella. She laughed that her preparation for going out in the rain consisted of a rain jacket and an umbrella that were in her car. However using them required remembering to bring either one or both for the rain. The streets were glistening from the street lights and the headlights from a passing car and she could hear the sloshing of the tires as they went by on the wet pavement. Beth was walking down the steps behind her as they were leaving the restaurant. They were still chatting as they never seemed to have enough time to talk about everything in their lives.

Beth was her best friend and confidant although they now saw each other only sporadically. When they talked, it was as though no time had passed since they had last seen each other. They had been friends for many years and the affection they felt for each other would never change. Alex had called Beth a number of times to get together, but she seemed busy with her life and spending time with her husband, Ben. Alex, who had never been married just believed that Beth was blissfully and happily married, spending time with her beloved husband and their friends. Alex was single without a significant other and she just did not fit in with Beth's social circle of couples. Alex observed that married couples felt uncomfortable having a single friend with them even though Beth tried to include Alex. That did not change their friendship and they still had no secrets between them. The geographical distance was not very far, but Alex worked many hours with her medical practice, seeing patients and performing surgeries. Beth was busy also, ensconced with her tennis, lunches and charity work. Alex was very pleased when Beth had suggested they meet for dinner at a fine local restaurant that had wonderful food. This was a perfect place to talk and catch up with what was happening in their lives.

They were happy to be together exchanging pleasantries while they ate. Alex was very observant and despite them talking incessantly and Beth seemingly cheerful, she noticed that tonight there was a sadness in Beth that had not been present in their previous conversations. They talked incessantly but Alex felt that there were things that Beth was not relating to her. It had been too long since they had a chance to talk undisturbed. Beth had been always been confident and happy and looked at life as a wonderful gift, but there was a cloud over this evenings conversation.

Beth was thinner with circles under her eyes. Beth started sobbing and began, "Ben has not been spending much time with me. This is a substantial change in our relationship. We were inseparable and talked frequently even when we're not together. I don't understand what happened or what I did to cause this distance between us." Alex was very distraught when she heard this and did not know what to say to Beth. She hoped that this was a temporary thing which was perhaps normal for married couples. She tried to cheer Beth up, hoping that this was a passing problem.

Beth was a small, petite blonde with even features and translucent flawless skin, beautiful on the outside as well as having a beautiful outlook on life. Alex respected Beth who was quick to complement people and make them feel good, never saying a mean thing about anyone. Beth met and fell in love with Ben while she was in college. It was like a fairy tale and their relationship quickly progressed to marriage. They had a small intimate wedding in a small chapel that was resplendently decorated with a myriad of white roses. Ben looked handsome in his suit, and Beth appeared angelic in her white dress with delicate lace at her bodice. A two week honeymoon to an island resort completed what Alex imagined to be the perfect marriage. Now Alex was shaken and distraught by what Beth told her.

Beth continued, "Ben has been criticizing everything I do. It wasn't major things at first but he has been belittling me and complaining about everything from my cooking to the way I dress. He never did this before." Alex used to see Beth once a week at least and spent afternoons together while Ben was working. She realized that in the past few months she and Beth had little communication and any conversations were brief. There was a change but she just believed that Beth was very busy.

Beth told Alex, "Ben is different. We have been like strangers and I don't understand why or what I am doing wrong. Once when we went dancing, he spent most of the time staring at someone he claimed was just a friend. He even commented that her skirt was too long to be attractive. This woman was voluptuous and cheap looking with long blonde dyed hair. Ben never did that before." She started crying.

Alex couldn't remember seeing Beth that upset. Beth was usually cheerful and happy, but this change was serious. Alex wondered if this had anything to do with the rumors she had heard from several mutual friends, that Livi, a friend of Ben's, had been saying terrible things about Beth to him and others else that would listen. Livi befriended Beth after she and Ben were together which gave her a chance to tell her terrible and untrue things about Ben. Livi even related that Beth frequently complained about Ben's lack of formal education and him being in a lower class than she was. Alex knew Beth very well and knew that she would never say any of those things. What Alex had heard from reliable sources was that Livi did frequently lie about people and things to get what she wanted. This almost sounded like Livi wanted Ben although she believed Ben already understood about Livi from all the years he knew her. Alex never told Beth about the rumors to avoid hurting her.

Beth continued, "He started coming home late and I even suggested marriage counseling but he said that was ridiculous. It just didn't make sense. I've been walking on eggshells, afraid to do anything because he found fault in everything I did. I was even afraid to talk to you because I feel that he wants the marriage to be over."

Alex didn't know what to say and just let Beth speak. Alex knew that Beth's money was in a trust and Ben couldn't get anything in a divorce, although she knew that didn't matter to Ben anyway.

Beth said, "We were partners in life and I was happy to be able to provide our wonderful lifestyle. I know his finances are more modest but that never meant anything to me because I love him and just want him to be happy. I thought we would be together forever."

Alex dwelled on what Beth said, but then a chill came down Alex's back when she realized that Ben would inherit everything if something happened to Beth. She did not say anything and didn't want to think about it because relationships sometimes have a rocky course, but they return to normal before long. She thought that Ben may have been under stress and wondered if he could have been going through a temporary financial drought from the downturn in the economy. Ben worked hard but sometimes that wasn't enough and it was common for people to take out their stress on the people they love.

Alex tried to allay Beth's fears and concern, "Isn't it possible that he was just working more hours because he is busy with business?"

"I don't know anything about it because he never discussed business with me" Alex didn't want to relate what she heard, especially because they were just rumors. There was no need to say anything to Beth and make her feel worse than she already did.

Alex continued, "Stop thinking it is your fault. You haven't done anything wrong. You used to talk to Livi often and when was the last time you talked to her?"

"It's a funny thing about that because she hasn't returned any of my phone calls or texts. We used to talk frequently for hours at a time and I just don't understand it. I know she is still in communication with Ben but he does not talk about their conversations. I even asked him how she is doing and he says only fine which makes me feel alienated. I am hurt and I don't understand why. "

Alex was very close to Beth and she was upset seeing her in so much pain. She tried to lighten the mood by talking about better things. She talked about some old the crazy fun things they did when they were roommates in school.

Alex said, "Do you remember when we were in college and decided to learn to drink alcohol as it showed we were sophisticated in social situations? Remember when we talked a friend into getting us a number of different alcoholic beverages and we got a book telling us how to mix drinks. One of the drinks called for the addition of powered sugar to the cocktail. It didn't matter how much we stirred but the powdered sugar kept settling on the bottom of the drink. We did not know enough that it was necessary to shake it or use a blender and only found out weeks later. We couldn't stop laughing when we heard that. It really did not matter because we couldn't drink much alcohol anyway so we gave up trying." They both started laughing.

"Then you and your boyfriend Claude took me to a fraternity party where the sweet gin drinks I was given tasted great and I couldn't taste the alcohol. I had too many of those drinks at the party and I became so drunk that I didn't remember that you and Claude took me home and you undressed me. I woke up the next morning with a terrible hangover, and I now know that term hangover is not nearly descriptive enough for how I felt. Since then, I can never look or think about drinking gin again." They laughed long and hard from the memory and it did help some to remove a lot of the tension from what Beth had said.

When they left the restaurant there was less tension and seeing Alex somehow made Beth feel better.

Still chatting, they started to cross the street when a car came speeding by. The car seemed to come out of nowhere and Alex had not seen the car coming towards them until Beth screamed. Alex reacted quickly and pulled Beth away to the safety between two parked cars. They both landed hard on the cement. The car kept going.

Alex asked, "Beth, are you hurt?" Alex was already visually scanning Beth while she talked, noticing that Beth was not moving quickly. Alex was moving slower as well but she ignored it and just grateful that they were not seriously injured.

Beth answered, "It is nothing that a few band aids won't cure." And she smiled weakly.

They looked at each other and started laughing which for some reason people do after a near death experience.

Alex mused thinking about people joking after emergencies or at funerals. Perhaps she thought it was to break the tension by making light of something to distract from the sadness of the occasion. Beth continued, "That was a close call. The driver must have been not paying attention. Do you think the driver was texting?"

They chuckled while Alex was helping Beth stand up, which was difficult at first. After brushing the muddy water from the ground from each other Alex started picking up the scattered contents from Beth's purse. She commented, "With all the things you have in your purse, I am surprised you forgot to bring the kitchen sink." They smiled at each other again. Beth had some bruises and scrapes but Alex was unscathed.

Still shaken and looking disheveled, they nodded assent to each other and they were ready to try to cross the wet, gleaming street to their cars. They looked both ways and saw no cars so they stepped off the curb. Alex was holding Beth's arm as she was little unsteady. Again Alex tried to lighten up what had happened and made a humorous remark. This time Beth stepped out first looking back at Alex laughing at what she said.

THE BOXES

With no warning and little noise on the pavement, a car sped over from the opposite direction and this time it seemed to be heading right for them. Alex didn't notice the car because had she was bending down to retrieve Beth's lipstick on the ground. Alex saw the car and screamed but it too late to grab Beth and pull her away. The car struck Beth directly, throwing her into the air and it caught Alex with the side of the bumper knocking her to the ground. Beth landed hard as did Alex, but Alex ignored her pain and managed to get over to Beth who wasn't moving. Alex bent over to check Beth while shouting to the people who were now standing around. "Call an ambulance!"

Alex found Beth to be unconscious but breathing with a strong regular heartbeat. She had a lot of bleeding from her right leg with broken bones sticking out, and Alex noticed that her right arm was badly broken as well. She didn't want to move her but Beth needed to have her neck stabilized in case it was broken. Alex looked up at the people standing around and shouted again, "I need some bricks or pillows or even some purses to keep her neck still, a belt and a flashlight or some matches."

The onlookers did not react right away and Alex shouted again. She did not look up at the person holding out the belt but thanked him while she put it securely on Beth's upper leg to stop the bleeding. The cigarette lighter a man handed her allowed Alex to check Beth's pupils and Alex was silently grateful that they were the same size and reacted equally to the light. Next she checked Beth's abdomen finding that it was distended and hard which was most likely from internal injuries.

Out of frustration, Alex called out, "Where is that ambulance?" She continued to check Beth and was somewhat relieved that the bleeding from her leg had decreased. Beth was still unconscious and now pale. With her medical training, Alex was able to think clearly and worked well in an emergency even though it involved her best friend.

The police cars with their flashing lights and sirens got there first, which they usually do, and they moved the crowd from around Beth. It seemed like a century to Alex before the ambulance pulled up although it had been only brief minutes.

Two paramedics came out of the ambulance, carrying the equipment they needed. They worked quickly, checking Beth while putting a collar around her neck and started an IV. The pulse oximeter they put on Beth's finger showed that her pulse was regular and she was getting enough oxygen.

After checking Beth, the taller paramedic looked up and asked" Who put this tourniquet on her leg?"

Alex had stepped back so that they could minister to Beth and replied "I did."

The tall paramedic looked up briefly at Alex and told her, "That was very good thinking, and you may have saved her life but we won't know her condition until we get her to the hospital"

As he and the other paramedic loaded Beth into the ambulance on a stretcher, Alex asked, "Can I accompany her to the hospital in the ambulance?"

The taller paramedic answered, "No ma'am, but you can see her at the hospital."

Alex looked at him and said, "But I am a doctor and her best friend. Can I go with her?"

Alex looked up at the clear blue eyes of the paramedic, noticing he was a nice-looking man. She immediately mentally chastised herself, as this was a true emergency and she's looking at a man. She surprised herself, because after her last real relationship had broken up she had no interest in dating or hanging out with anyone.

THE BOXES

The paramedic now actually looked at Alex, just as the lights from the ambulance lit up her face. He noticed her even features, clear sea green eyes, with long dark hair falling over her shoulders. Without thinking he said "You are a doctor?" He thought to himself, she is absolutely beautiful and does not realize it. She looks more like an actress. He continued, "It doesn't matter that you are a doctor because we don't carry passengers, even doctors. We need to monitor her closely and you can see her at the hospital." He continued to treat Beth after she was in the ambulance thinking that he was looking forward to seeing Alex again.

THE BOXES

CHAPTER 2

ALEX IN WAITING ROOM

Alex was surprised that she able to drive even though she was injured and shaken up. She kept going through what had happened in her mind. She still couldn't believe it, and kept trying to think if there was anything she could have done to avoid Beth's injuries. Leaving for the hospital, she realized that she was distracted and driving erratically. It made her chuckle to think of what she would say to a policeman who pulled her over and try to explain the blood all over her. She smiled thinking it was a good thing she didn't have a bloody axe in the car.

On her way to the hospital, Alex called Ben both on his cell and at home to tell him that Beth was in an accident and on her way to the hospital. She left several messages and asked him to call her right away. Fortunately the hospital was close and the paramedics quickly moved Beth into the emergency room.

THE BOXES

Once at the hospital, Alex knew that she would only get in the way in the Emergency room when the doctors and staff there worked on Beth. She knew they would draw blood, check her heart, get X-rays, and type her blood for a transfusion. Beth's abdomen was hard and Alex expected that they would check her abdomen for any internal injuries. Beth was also very pale and Alex was sure that she needed a transfusion, surgery for her broken leg and for her abdominal injury. The fracture of her arm also needed to be treated. Alex knew what the procedures were by the benefit of her training and that the doctors in the emergency room where they were took Beth, were very competent. Beth would be in good hands.

Alex walked into the crowded waiting room at the emergency department and she knew that there was nothing she could do now but wait. She reacted well and knowledgeably in the emergency but now her emotions overwhelmed her. She sat down in a quiet, secluded part of the waiting room and started to cry. She chuckled at herself thinking that here she was crying and acting like a woman. She reminded herself that she WAS a woman. Alex was dazed and didn't know how long she was there but she was worried about Beth.

THE BOXES

When the tall paramedic, Mike, found Alex in the waiting room, he said, "You were difficult to find. What are you doing sitting in the waiting room? You may be a doctor, but you should know that you also need to be seen and treated by the doctors in the emergency room." Alex nodded in agreement and tried to muster a smile. When she tried to stand up she didn't realize how unsteady she was and the paramedic grabbed her by the shoulders and sat her down again. He told her, "Wait right here." Alex did not protest and it was only then that she looked down at herself noticing how disheveled she was, and covered in blood. She now noticed the people in the waiting room looking at her although no one had said anything. The paramedic came back with a wheelchair, gently sat her down in the chair and wheeled her into the emergency room.

Of course Alex knew the doctors and nurses in the emergency room who acknowledged her when she was wheeled in. Alex looked up at Mike and all that she could say was a simple, "Thank you." She was grateful for the attention and thoughtfulness of this paramedic, mentally noting that besides being good looking, he was also caring. What was she thinking? This is ridiculous because it was his job to do this for anyone who needed help

THE BOXES

As Mike was rolling her past the intake desk into the treatment area in the emergency room, he said to her, "I wanted to apologize for acting surprised that you are a doctor. It was a surprise because I don't see female doctors that are this pretty." He smiled a wide smile that showed even white teeth, lighting up his face with his smile.

Alex smiled and commented, "Thank you for the complement." She knew she looked like she had been in an accident but at least she felt less tense. Once again, despite what she had been through, she again noticed that he was very attractive.

The paramedic blushed, "Call me Mike, and you are doctor....?"

Alex tried to smile and replied, "Call me Alex and what you said is no problem."

As Alex was wheeled back, the triage nurse in the emergency looked at Alex covered in blood and said "Who won the fight?" They both chuckled as the nurse now took Alex to the back where she helped her onto a patient cart. The nurse cursorily checked Alex to see if she was badly hurt and needed immediate attention to any injury. Finding nothing critical, she put Alex into a hospital gown after gently removing her shoes and clothing. The nurse looked her over again, noticing she didn't seem to be in distress and said, "Hello Dr Marsh, I would ask about how you are doing but your appearance is telling". Alex laughed weakly, thinking about her appearance. The nurse continued, "Let's go over what happened. Are you in any pain?"

Alex tried not to be funny and rejected answering that she was good considering she had been run down by a car. She replied, "I had an altercation with a car bumper but I don't have much pain." She knew but didn't say that often patients in shock have little or no pain. She had been through a lot, seeing her best friend badly injured right in front of her, but not enough for her to go into shock, or hopefully not.

The nurse smiled and said, "It's good to see you although the circumstances could be better. Your doctor will be in shortly." She made sure Alex was comfortable and very gently started sponging away the blood.

Alex said trying to lighten the mood, "Not all of this blood is mine. You should see the other guy." Alex looked at the nurse who did not smile. Alex hoped it was because she didn't hear the remark although she knew that not everyone got her sense of humor. Alex continued, "Most of the blood is from my best friend Beth who was just brought in by ambulance. She was struck by the same car that hit me and how is she doing?"

The nurse was evasive following the privacy policy regarding other patients but she did say "Beth is being evaluated and I don't know any more than that." She could see the worried look on Alex's face and commented, "Beth is in the right place and I am sure they are doing everything they can to help her."

Alex knowing that Beth's injuries were severe and seeing no call from Ben on her cell phone, inquired, "Has Beth's husband called?"

"I don't know but that does not mean that he hasn't called. Your friend is in another area in the emergency room and there are a lot of personnel there."

Alex wondered why Ben hadn't at least called her cell phone about Beth after all of the messages she had left for him. She wondered why he did not call back right away as he would have finished work by now. He should have answered and at least been on his way to the hospital or here already. There was nothing she could do now.

After was glad she survived reasonably intact and was worrying about Beth, waiting for the doctor to come into her cubicle, when a man came in. Alex's cubicle. He was a large man with a protruding belly and his hair was combed over to one side, probably trying to hide his baldness. He was a little short of breath most likely from not being used to hurrying through a large hospital. He was unshaven and wearing a suit that did not fit him, with his tie loose. He introduced himself as Detective Schultz, flashed his detective badge, and asked if he could ask her some questions about what happened. Alex nodded assent and he sat down pulling out a note pad. "We are investigating the hit and run accident of which you and your friend Beth were victims. We want to know what happened and I would like to get as much information as you can remember, while it is fresh in your mind."

Alex looked at him and thought about the term the detective used, 'fresh'? She smiled at herself while joking in her mind that this was the first time she had been called fresh. She chided herself to stop going on a tangent and trying to be funny because this was very serious.

Alex was shaken trying to remember the accident and the injury, still regretting not getting to Beth fast enough to pull her away the second time a car came towards them. Now with questions about the accident, she remembered and realized that there was not a blinding light or a screech of brakes before she and Beth were struck. The headlights of the car that hit them were off, as well as with the first car that almost hit them. Her concern turned to fright as she started thinking that this was no accident because the car seemed to be aiming for she and Beth.

The Detective also questioned in his mind if this was an accident although he did not say anything. He had been told by the police investigating the accident scene, that a car had narrowly missed them the first time it went by, but they were struck when a car came by again from the opposite direction. He wondered if the same car had been targeting them twice and the second time injuring them.

Alex mustered a smile to try to lessen the stress and weakly, said, "You can ask questions as long as I am not going to be graded on my answers. And no one has called me fresh in a long time."

The detective smiled and said, "I guess your mental functions are good because the first thing to go is a sense of humor." Alex chuckled even though it was painful to laugh and she realized she would have bruises all over. He continued, "Let's start and what do you remember?"

THE BOXES

"Beth and I left the restaurant where we had dinner and had just stepped into the street when a car sped towards us. I pulled her out of the way to avoid the car the first time when she sustained some abrasions and some bruises from falling on the pavement."

"So you and she weren't badly injured the first time the car went by. Then what happened?"

"We were only bruised and shaken up the first time so we decided to try to cross the street again to get to our cars. That was when a car came at us again when Beth was hit directly, and I was struck by part of the bumper. Beth was badly injured and I tried to help her at the scene."

"Was there any warning before this happened?"

Alex thought about it and said, "There was no warning, no screeching of brakes and the headlights were off on the car that hit us. Actually the headlights were off both times." She shuddered at this realization.

The detective took notes, and asked, "Was it the same car both times?"

Alex answered, "I'm not sure. I think we were too busy getting injured to notice the car that struck us." She thought she had to stop with her humor, even though it lightened things up. This was serious.

The detective pretended not to hear her remark. "How fast did you think the car was going?"

Alex smiled and said nothing, trying to stop herself from making a remark that the car was going about the speed of a low flying airplane. "I'm don't know"

Detective Schultz said, "Now this is going to be hard."

Alex mentally caught herself thinking that whatever he said was hard was not as hard as the bumper of the car that hit them. She thought again that she had to stop and be serious.

Detective Schultz continued, "Do you believe this was an accident?"

"I don't know and I did not have time to think about it", although her mind was screaming that it was not an accident.

"Is there anyone that you or Beth know that would try to hurt you or her?"

Alex immediately regretted after she said this, "Beth said that she and her husband Ben were having a few marital problems but nothing serious. He would never harm her." Alex just realized that she made Ben a suspect for what happened. However, she knew that they would not find anything wrong. Lots of married couples had problems and something like this was a bit extreme.

Her nurse smiled, checked her vital signs and said the doctor will be in shortly.

Alex added, "I am starting to get a little fuzzy, so can we continue this another time?"

"No problem and feel better." He stood up and left, thinking that what happened was a shame, especially since they could not find any witnesses to what happened.

Dr Katz walked into the exam room and said to Alex "Well I guess I've seen you look better. You look like you were hit by a truck."

Alex replied, "I guess the truck won this altercation, although it was a car. It felt more like a Sherman tank." They both laughed at Alex's remark.

Dr Katz commented, "Well this is a good sign. You haven't lost your sense of humor."

He continued, "Well you know the drill. We are going to get x-rays, blood work CT, and with the large knot on the side of your head, you probably have a concussion. You are also going to need some suturing for the multiple lacerations including the one on your forehead. With a probable concussion, you know we are also keeping you here." Great, thought Alex thinking that now she was going to know what her patients feel like.

A cosmetic surgeon Alex knew was called in to do the suturing to minimize the scaring from her lacerations. Alex looked at the surgeon while he was suturing her and commented, "Don't worry, I won't grade you on your suturing." They both chuckled at this, and of course Alex could not help saying, "Will a scar from the laceration on my forehead mean that I could be mistaken for a boy wizard?" The surgeon and Alex actually laughed at this, knowing that the scar would not even be visible once it healed.

The neurologist she knew ordered a cat scan of her head after he looked at her head injury. Shortly afterwards, Dr. Katz came in to report that her tests were normal. Alex was trying to think clearly about everything that had happened. She knew that it was just a matter of time before SHE would become the patient. She asked, "How is Beth doing?"

Dr Katz reported, "She was conscious and stable before she went into surgery and I am not certain when she will be out. I heard you helped her a lot after your accident. However, you are the patient now."

THE BOXES

Alex was relieved that she had passed inspection except for needing her abrasions dressed and the lacerations sewn. All of her tests were good but she was admitted and placed in a hospital room for observation for at least one night, depending on her condition.

CHAPTER 3

BETH TO SURGERY AND HISTORY

Beth was lucky to be alive although Alex knew her condition was very serious. At least Beth was conscious before her surgery, which was a good sign and fortunately she was in a great place to be treated.

Now in her hospital room, Alex had a chance to think about Beth and her relationship with Ben. Beth had a loving family and a happy childhood with parents who saw to it that she wanted for nothing. Her father had a very large manufacturing business which allowed them to live in a large house with many employees. When Beth was young, she loved the cook, Magda who came from 'the old country', although Beth did not know where that was. Magda had a thick accent and Beth did not always understand her but Magda always listened to Beth's experiences and nodded in approval. Beth loved her pork roast and Magda always made it for her birthday or any special occasion. The kitchen was large and warm from the ovens and always smelled of wonderful foods being cooked. Beth also loved her maid even though she chided Beth for leaving clothing on the floor or trying to go out without enough warm clothing on chilly days. They saw each other often in the large vacuous house and laughed a lot about the others working in the house.

Their chauffeur, Dave was always polite to Beth but he did give her advice about tolerating her classmates who had been unkind to her. Beth was a sweet, kind child and did not understand why anyone criticized her at school. Dave believed that her classmates may have been jealous because of where she lived and that she was beautiful. She had long blonde hair that shined in the sunlight, with rosy cheeks and lips that were naturally red. He tried to make Beth feel better and often reassured her that it was not really anything that she did. Beth was a mediocre student but she made up for it with a cheery disposition, smiling most of the time with no malice towards anyone. Beth was never short of dates for the school dances including her prom, but she never got close to any of the boys that showed her attention.

Beth's parents celebrated her graduation with a lavish party and she went to the same expensive university her parents had attended. Despite being pretty with beautiful, stylish clothing and an expensive car, she never felt like she fit in with the other students. Then when she met Alex, who was her roommate in college on an academic scholarship, they became best friends. Alex was an excellent student, planning to go to medical school and she helped Beth get through her classes. They laughed a lot and just enjoyed the time they spent together, talking frequently about what they wanted to do when they graduated. Beth figured that she would get married and have a lot of children, but Alex only had aspirations of becoming a doctor. She was a science nerd who never took the time to put on makeup or dress in anything but functional clothing, which was the polar opposite to Beth. Alex was tall with dark hair and never believed she was pretty.

Beth was a pretty, petite blonde with a good figure and a cheery disposition. Beth was the kind of girl that men were immediately attracted to and despite being asked out for dates frequently, she never had a boyfriend. It was during her first year of graduate school when she unexpectedly bumped into a very attractive man at one of the local pubs frequented by students. He introduced himself to her as Ben and was well dressed confident, unlike anyone else she had ever met. Ben was very tall, dark and handsome, slim but with large shoulders, a very sexy man. He was witty and very bright even though he never had a formal education. His upbringing was very modest and he became a race car mechanic but also started a few businesses that were doing well financially.

Ben liked to dance and he paid for dancing lessons for her. They went to a lot of clubs to dance where she met a lot of people he knew, and he made Beth feel special. She could tell that a number of the women there wanted to be with him, but he chose her. Beth felt she was pretty but not beautiful and was grateful for the attention of this handsome, worldly man. Ben was a gentleman and made sure he spent a lot of time with her except for when she had classes or was studying. They went to the gym together and she exercised while he played basketball with his friends. They had breakfast and lunch together every day, and they even went to each other's doctors together. He cooked her dinner often making sure she ate a healthy diet. All of his friends welcomed her and told her that they had never seen him happier. She was euphoric and loved him unconditionally.

THE BOXES

He finally introduced her to who he described as his closest friend Livia, or Livi as everyone called her. Livi and Beth became friends talking frequently, and started spending time together. Beth did not notice Livi's reaction when she and Ben were together. She was usually astute, but never realized how upset Livia was that Ben wanted to be with her and not Livi. Ben barely paid attention to Livi to talk to Beth when they socialized. Now, under the guise of friendship, Livi started telling her Ben was wrong for her, not educated or intelligent enough, in a lower class, and a womanizer with ex-girlfriends everywhere. Beth did not pay attention to what Livi said about Ben. It did not make sense to her that Livi was such a close friend of Ben's and yet she said so many terrible things about him. Just being with Ben dispelled all of Beth's insecurities she had lived with her whole life and he was everything she ever wanted in a significant other. Alex had never seen two people happier together and she was very pleased for Beth.

Beth moved into Ben's place which was very modest but she felt it was perfect for them because she didn't care where they were, as long as they were together. They soon got married and they seemed ideal for each other. The party for their first anniversary was large and lavish and Beth was happy.

Ben never knew her background before they got married, and it didn't matter to him when he found out that she came from a very wealthy family.

They were married almost two years when her parents passed away. Her father was poorly compliant with the treatment for his high blood pressure which contributed to and may have caused the abdominal aneurysm that burst before he could be saved. It was only six months later, that her mother was found to have pancreatic cancer. Her doctors could not say how long her mother had it, but the tumor was very large and had metastasized before she felt any abdominal pain. Unfortunately that history is not uncommon for pancreatic cancer. Her mother was told that the metastases had spread to a number of organs including her liver and that she had maybe 6 months to live. She was still grieving for Beth's father and refused to have the chemotherapy that her doctors recommended. Beth was devastated because she had lost both of her parents only six months apart. She knew she was lucky that Ben was there with her through these life shattering tragedies.

THE BOXES

Beth inherited everything from her parents who had placed their assets in a trust for her. She was now a very wealthy woman but that wasn't important to her. Her only thoughts were about Ben and making him happy. Beth convinced Ben to move into a very elegant home that was made possible by her trust even though she knew that material things did not matter to him. Beth wanted to have children right away but he said he wanted to wait and she trusted his judgement.

Now Beth was in the emergency room, regaining consciousness. She looked around, not realizing where she was except that she was in pain. Her memory started coming back and she was hurting all over. She now remembered her terror when she was struck by the car and realized that Ben wasn't with her now. She was panicking and kept asking the nurses, "Where is Ben? Why isn't he here?"

The nurses tried to calm her which only worked somewhat and then her doctor came in, "You need to go to surgery because you apparently have some bleeding in your abdomen, and to treat a broken leg. What is most important is for you to relax so that you can get better."

THE BOXES

Beth realized that he was trying to help her, but she asked him, "Where is my husband Ben? Are there any messages on my cell phone or has he called?"

Her doctor replied, "I haven't heard anything but you need to concentrate on getting better." He didn't know what to say to her but he tried to keep her cheerful.

Beth was now silent, not knowing what to think because recently she sometimes had trouble reaching Ben. She was worried about Alex and asked anxiously, "How is Alex doing?"

The nurse standing by the bed said, "Alex was not hurt badly and I think she is in the waiting room, worried about you. You are due in surgery now and you can see her when you wake up."

Beth quipped, "This hasn't been a good day." And she smiled weakly as they wheeled her into the surgical suite.

THE BOXES

Chapter 4

Alex visitors- call Pete

Alex was admitted and evaluated by the nurses while lying in her hospital bed. Of course, they checked her pupils frequently to make sure she had no other concerns besides her concussion. She was very unsteady when she tried to walk so she was confined to her bed. Alex overlooked her injuries as she was still very worried about Beth. She was relieved when a nurse who was a friend stopped by to tell her that that Beth had come out of surgery all right, but she was still sleeping from the anesthetic. Beth was placed in a bed in the Intensive care unit of the hospital and could not receive any visitors except family. Of course being a staff doctor, Alex could see her anytime but not until she was able to walk steadier than a three year old which made her chuckle to herself. She wondered where Beth's husband was because she still hadn't heard from him.

THE BOXES

Alex's hospital room was neat and clean, very white and some the nurses stopped by to see her as they knew her from her patients that she admitted. She was deep in thought when she had a welcome visitor.

Mike, the tall, attractive paramedic came to the door and knocked on the door frame. He asked," Are you dressed?"

Alex smiled, "It depends on whether you call a hospital gown being dressed. At least they gave me two gowns so both my front and back are covered." They chuckled and she answered, "Come on in. I'll see if I can fit you into my busy schedule."

"You are looking a little better than the last time I saw you." He commented and smiled. "I just wanted to stop by and see if you are alright." He was carrying flowers and a box of candy.

Alex was pleased and indicated for him to sit in the chair close to her bed and said, "I appreciate your visit and thank you for the gifts."

"I just wanted to cheer you up?"

Alex smiled. "I am fine, about as good as a person with a concussion can be. Since a concussion can make you not think clearly, I guess I can say or do anything and use my concussion as an excuse." Alex thought that he is a nice man, "I am as good as can be while being confined to a hospital bed and this is a nice touch having a follow up by a paramedic from the accident. How are you?"

"I am good but I am not the one in the hospital. You seem to be in good spirits and at least I didn't have to bring a body bag."

She was attracted to him, slim but muscular with bright blue eyes and attentive. She thought that he is a good man and actually the first man she had even noticed in a very long time. Other men had paid attention to her and wanted to go out with her, but she had no interest in getting involved. She agreed only to spend time with them as a friend. She supposed that it would take time for her to consider anything beyond friendship as her trust level in men had been painfully removed from her consciousness.

Alex inquired, "Have you been busy?"

Mike smiled. "Yes, saving lives, putting out forest fires, and only one doctor to save today. Actually I just finished my shift and I am skipping my classes tonight."

Alex was surprised, "Classes? What classes are you taking?"

"I am working on an MBA in business as I don't plan to be a paramedic forever although it does pay the bills while I am in school."

"That is very ambitious." And she respected this man a lot thinking that just maybe she should consider going out with him if he asked. She thought, wait a minute, I am getting ahead of myself. She didn't even know if he was interested in being anything more than being a friend. Thinking that way surprised her.

Mike continued, "I admit that this was an unusual way to meet and does this count as a rescue?" They both laughed.

Alex hesitated and smiled, "I guess this counts and are we keeping score?"

"Why not, especially when I find a female doctor to save or help." They both smiled. "How long will they be keeping you held hostage here?"

"I might be able go home in a day or two with good behavior and actually I am hoping doc Katz won't keep me too long."

Mike asked, "When you get discharged, can I give you a ride home? I will have time and I would like to do that." That made her feel good.

"I appreciate that and one of my staff was going to take me when I can go, but I will take you up on your offer."

Mike asked, "Hospitals are a tough place to be and are you able to get any rest?"

"These fine nurses will make certain I am awake every hour when they check me which you know is the protocol for concussion patients. They check me for irregular pupil size but of course you already know that." She laughed again. "As you see, I am just finishing the gourmet cuisine they call dinner."

"I thought about picking up some food for you but I am glad you already had something to eat."

"I am glad you came by and my staff will probably come by to check on me. They were concerned and wanted to know how I thought I could take on a speeding car." They both laughed out loud at this remark.

Talking to Mike was easy and he was also very attractive. Alex was now curious to know more about him and asked, "Where do you come from?"

"Dallas Texas, born and bred."

"But you don't have an accent, a Texas drawl."

He chuckled. "That is a stereotype and notice that am not wearing a hat and boots either."

Embarrassed, she tried to explain, "I didn't mean to say....."

He said, "Don't worry about it because you are not the only one that says that.....y'all." They both laughed again. Alex thought she always liked a person with a sense of humor, which she now realized that her adulterous ex fiancé did not have.

Alex felt comfortable with Mike and enjoyed his company. She added, "I am ready to go home now but I have to stay until my doctor says I can go. I did hit my head pretty hard and I am still dizzy. They told me that I couldn't drive for a week after I was discharged because of my concussion, but as you probably know, doctors are the worst patients so I will see."

They both laughed at her comment. The conversation was pleasant and they joked about a lot of trivial things which was just what Alex needed right now. She knew the impact of what happed to her and Beth hadn't fully affected her yet.

Mike continued, "I know the staff is competent and the hospital food isn't too bad. After all that you have gone through, I know you need rest. If it is alright I will come by tomorrow and let me know when you are going to be discharged. Good night."

Alex was grateful for his visit. "I am pretty exhausted. Thank you for your help and the gifts."

Mike smiled and said on his way out, "Goodnight and try to get some sleep."

Alex now had time to think about her conversation with Beth and all the fears she had about her relationship with her husband. Alex always believed that Beth and her husband were in love, and had a wonderful marriage. This concerned her because Beth was her best friend and had been having doubts for a long time but never said anything to her. Beth had been reluctant to talk to her and she wondered if there was something going on that Beth didn't want to face until now. Alex didn't want to think about that when they were both in the hospital recovering.

After Mike left, she called Ben and this time he answered his phone. "We tried to reach you but couldn't. Where were you?"

After a short pause, Ben replied, "I've been very busy with work lately."

"Have you been by the hospital to see Beth and when did you hear about her being hit by a car?

"I talked to her doctor and I am on my way to the hospital now. Are you alright?" Alex was relieved that he finally answered and was coming to see Beth.

"I am ok and I know Beth will be very happy to see you."

"I am almost there and feel better."

Alex could tell that Ben was distressed and it was from more than Beth's injury. Her conversation was short with Ben and he did not seem upset about what happened. One of the skills that Alex had acquired from her years of medical training and practice was that she could tell when someone was lying. Beth was her best friend whom she loved her dearly, but something was wrong. Alex wanted to protect Beth and help her find out why there was a change in her and Ben's relationship.

Alex called Pete who was one of her patients and had become a close friend. He was a highly respected private investigator and she thought it was a good idea to hire him for what was going on with Beth, as well as look into their car altercation. It was late but she knew he didn't mind.

When he answered his phone, Alex asked, "Pete, how have you been and how's business?"

Pete replied, "Busy as ever, and I am so swamped with work and I am considering taking in an associate. How are you and how's the practice? It's very nice hearing from you and where are you? "

"I am ripening in a hospital bed recovering from a concussion."

"Oh no! What happened and why didn't you call me? Do you want me to come see you?"

"It is not necessary" she replied. "I am sorry I did not call you earlier but I am receiving excellent care, maybe too good" and she laughed which relieved some of Pete's concern. She related the events that got her there.

Pete was thinking, "I am happy to hear you are alright. You know I worry about you, and as much as it is always a pleasure to hear from you, I have a feeling that you are calling for more than just catching up. Do you need my help with this?"

"You always were astute and I am very concerned about Beth, her marriage and what happened today. We met for dinner before the accident, if that's what it was, and she related to me that she was having marital problems. We couldn't reach him for a long time when her injury happened but when I did talk to him just now, he told me he was working. I could tell he wasn't telling the truth."

She continued, "Apparently according to Beth, he has been working late a lot and hadn't spent much time with her. She said there was a substantial change in their relationship which seemed to happen somewhat quickly."

Pete thought about what she said. "So you want to find out why there was a change and why he is out a lot. What are you thinking?"

'I am not sure but something is not right. I am also concerned because I do not believe that what happened was an accident."

"I have been doing this too long and I know what you're thinking. I assume you want to know what has been occupying Ben's time and look into what happened. When do you want me to start?" Pete was concerned about Beth.

"Yesterday." And they both chuckled.

Pete continued, "I understand and you know you're in good hands. Give me all the details and I will start tomorrow." This relieved Alex somewhat as it was best to know what is going on.

Alex was relaxing when Dr Raymond came in and asked, "How are you feeling?"

"Fine, bored and I don't do this patient stuff well."
They both laughed.

He went on, "Everything is alright but we want to keep
you a few days for observation, especially since you hit
your head pretty hard and you are dizzy.

"I will try to be a good patient." They both smiled.

Alex had a headache and was sore everywhere, but
otherwise felt all right. There was not enough for her to do
as her mind was still active. Just as she was ready to watch
a boring game show on TV, she heard a knock at her door.
She looked over and said, "Come in." Cassie, her friend
and office manager, and her staff walked in carrying candy,
flowers and a get well balloon. Alex smiled, grateful for the
company which made her feel good.

Cassie was worried and asked "Are you alright?" Alex
had a hard working staff who cared about her patients as
she and they had fun working there. Her staff were more
like friends and family which in addition to Alex's skill,
made the practice very busy. Alex rewarded her staff's
dedication and hard work by taking all of them to medical
meetings with her, to places like San Diego, Las Vegas,
Washington, and DC, where they had a great time. And of
course they always reminded the boss that she should take

time off for personal vacations which involved having a personal life. Alex agreed with them and responded I will sometime.

Cassie was trying to be cheerful to take Alex's mine off of her injuries, "Do you remember when we were in Las Vegas the week of the national rodeo competitions and the night we decided to see the rodeo?"

They all looked at each other and started chuckling. Alex replied, "Yes I do...."

Cassie reminisced, "There were all of these tall, good looking cowboys walking around the hotel and by the arena where you were walking around by yourself. The rest of us were just coming towards you from the gift shop when this tall hunk of a cowboy walked up to you and started talking.

"We heard him say, 'You are mighty purty' and he took his hat off to put it on your head and commented, 'It looks a lot better on you 'ma'am' than on me.' He was smiling and he asked if you would like to watch him in the bull riding competition shortly. We all agreed for you. It was an education watching him and the other cowboys after which he invited all of us to celebrate his win. Boy did we celebrate."

THE BOXES

Alex was smiling, thinking about how much fun they had. "It was late and I remember him asking to see me again, but I don't remember how much we had to drink or how we got back to our hotel."

Cassie answered, "He took us to our hotel and he did call the next day, but not too early thank goodness. You were already at one of the lectures and I still don't know how you did that."

Alex was still smiling, "Yes I made it, but the volume of the speaker was substantially louder than it was the day before."

They started laughing so hard they were almost crying and Cassie finally said to all of them, "Well I guess we need to let our boss lady, isn't that what the cowboy called you, get some rest."

Alex was more cheerful when they said goodnight and left. There was not much for her to do now but she was still not sleepy and there was nothing good on TV. This gave her too much time to think and her thoughts turned to her past relationships, her broken engagement and cookie man. Cookie man was the nickname her friends had for Sal which always made her smile and brought a wave of happy memories.

THE BOXES

Alex was able to sleep very little as the nurses were checking her every hour. This made her remember her days as a resident when she was so sleep deprived, that she joked that she could fall asleep standing up. Alex was looking forward to going home and getting real sleep. She couldn't do much for the next few days anyway as she was told she could not drive for a week because of her concussion. Work was also supposed to be prohibited which made her smile because she knew she was not was going to follow these instructions. After all, doctors are the worst patients.

Lying in her hospital bed, the adrenaline from the day's activities wore off and Alex slept when she could. She smiled and thought, so much for the sleep that a patient needs after being injured in a near-death experience. Despite sleep deprivation and during the short time she did sleep, she was surprised that she was able to dream. Unfortunately she dreamed about Larry, her former fiancé, which made her remember how badly she was hurt by him. She tried to forget what had happened.

THE BOXES

CHAPTER 5

ALEX HOSPITAL-HISTORY LARRY

The next morning Alex was feeling better although still confined to her hospital bed, she happy to hear that Beth's surgery went well. Perhaps it was the quiet or just having had a close brush with death, that caused Alex to start reflecting on her life. She felt lucky to be a surgeon, although she did work very hard in college and medical school to achieve that. Alex was an only child whose upbringing was very modest with older parents who provided her clothing and sustenance. Her parents did feel blessed to finally have a child after years of trying, especially since they could not afford the special procedures to conceive a child that some couples could afford.

Alex did not grow up with any luxuries although she had a good home and everything she needed. She never cared about the extra things that some of her friends had. What mattered to her were the many plants that she had acquired by cuttings or what someone else no longer wanted, and animals that she had rescued or adopted. She was grateful to her parents who provided for her, but she was never given much affection. Alex was fortunately an excellent student and remarkably knew from a young age that she wanted to be a doctor. Her mother was a secretary and her father worked for an insurance agency which enabled them to pay for some of her school tuition, doing so by denying themselves simple luxuries that they otherwise could have enjoyed. Alex was thankful for having been given the opportunity to accomplish what she did. She was quiet and shy but she did notice the closeness and affection in the families of the few friends she had. Their parents hugged them and said they loved them which Alex never received from her parents. She recalled the difference in her later life during quiet times. She was always trying to please her parents with perfect grades and never getting into trouble but it just seemed to be expected.

Alex was thin and tall for her age, gangly and athletic although she did not participate in team sports. Despite her parents suggesting that she participate in school activities even though she was very shy and uncomfortable in social situations. The only clubs she did join were for math and science. Alex used to observe the popular students who flirted and interacted with others, which made her feel like an outsider. Intelligence did not matter to this crowd but she become friends with two fellow students who also excelled academically. As her mother did not care about fashion, the clothes Alex wore were modest and practical which did not attract any attention to her. When her parents asked Alex about what she wanted to do to celebrate her birthday with her friends or classmates, her choice was to go to the zoo or to science museums.

Alex never knew the whole story about her parent's death which happened when she was a freshman in college, except that she was told it was in a plane crash and she was too devastated to question it. There was a modest amount of money from the sale of the family home that paid for the funerals, and what was left was combined with her academic scholarship to college, she was able to attend medical school. Her roommate and close friend Beth, along with Alex's academic counselor, gave her guidance and emotional support. Without them, Alex would never have finished college or gone to medical school. She progressed to have a very successful practice doing ear, nose and throat surgery.

THE BOXES

Now she was confined to her hospital bed with a concussion and one of her colleagues Fred was covering for her while she was here. Of course he had to say, "You would do anything to get a day off. And you could still do consultations while you are here in the hospital. Patients won't notice or care that you are in a hospital gown with an IV." She laughed.

He always did make her laugh and she commented, "That's ok but I do look like I lost the fight with a speeding car."

Fred always appreciated her humor and said, "Feel better. I will drop by to say hi and to check on you. Do you need anything?"

Alex thought, a steak, mashed potatoes, Caesar salad, and cheesecake for desert, but she replied, "No but thanks, and I appreciate you covering for me. I will get back to work in a few days."

Fred commented, "There is no rush. Feel better."

"Thanks." She was grateful for Fred who covered for her.

Alex was now in her hospital bed thinking about Beth, grateful that she was getting better. At first she had been a little envious but actually happy that Beth had found someone wonderful to be with and be that much in love. Alex's relationships were fleeting after Larry, except for the impossible relationship with Sal which only seemed like a dream. She just wasn't emotionally ready for involvement.

She remembered what had happened with her ex-fiancé Larry too well. She would never have gotten involved with Sal if she had not been traumatized by what happened with Larry.

She was the middle of her junior year in college, when Larry came up to her in the library and introduced himself. He had no idea who she was, although she knew well who he was, her crush from high school. Larry was two years ahead of Alex, tall and handsome, class president and the captain of the football team. Of course his girlfriend in high school was the beautiful buxom blonde, the captain of the cheerleading squad. Alex was a plain, skinny nerd that he never noticed her and even when he sat behind her in chemistry. None of the other boys in school paid any attention to her either and she felt like she had the sex appeal of wallpaper. Even though she was often described as very intelligent, it did not matter to her at the time. She observed the boys in school who followed around flirting with the pretty girls and in her mind she kept thinking, 'I am smart but why couldn't I be pretty!'

By the time Alex started college, she had filled out a great deal and had transformed from a plain nerd into a very attractive woman. In her mind she still thought of herself as the plain skinny nerd she had been before. She was a very dedicated student, preparing to go to medical school and did not have time or the interest to date. When she and Larry met and started talking he asked, "We really went to high school together? Alex smiled and wasn't surprised as none of her fellow male students noticed her either. After conversing for a while he asked, "Would you like to join me for lunch?" She felt like melting as she was not only noticed, but asked for lunch by her high school crush.

She barely was able to muster, "Yes."

Larry was clever and funny during lunch and she was able to relax. They were talking for two hours and when they finished, he asked if he could see her again. She agreed and was in disbelief. She couldn't wait to call Beth to tell her and ask her for advice on what to wear and what to do since she had little experience with dating.

THE BOXES

Fortunately, Beth's help was not needed since Alex and Larry were very comfortable spending time together, laughing and talking. Alex never really knew him in high school and she was impressed that he was intelligent and funny as well as being very handsome. He appreciated that Alex was special and not just pretty, but intelligent and fun to be with. She was different from the other women he had dated.

They started seeing each other frequently and got very close, becoming a couple. Larry was her first boyfriend and they were affectionate, held hands, kissed and Larry made sure everyone knew they were together. He was everything that Alex could want in a boyfriend. Larry told her often that he loved her and she was certain that they would have a perfect life together. He gave her flowers for her birthday, Valentine's Day, and whenever he thought she needed cheering up.

Larry graduated first and started law school at the same university so that they could still be together. After he got his law degree he planned to do a year of legal specialization to become a trial attorney.

Alex was and excellent student, finishing college in three years and attended medical school at the same university. They studied together and spent what little time they had free together. He was recruited by the most prestigious law firm in the area that specialized in litigation, requiring him to work many hours. Alex had three years left in her residency which required her to work many hours as well but they still saw each other as often as possible. Larry went to her hospital parties with her and she was at his law firm functions.

Alex was concerned that their many hours working, including the nights that Alex had to go into the hospital, might cause them to grow apart. Larry assured her that everything was fine and not to worry. After being together for two years they discussed marriage but Larry wanted to wait until the right time.

Alex trusted his judgement and she lived for the precious times she could be with him. Larry was the first and only person she had ever loved.

Alex remembered one beautiful evening in May when the flowers were blooming and the trees and grass had turned green. It had been raining the day before but now the weather was warm with clear skies and a gentle breeze. Alex had finished making rounds on the patients early so she had time to shower and change to meet Larry. He made reservations for them at the charming French restaurant where they had eaten on her birthday. Alex kept telling herself how lucky she was having Larry in her life.

The room was dimly lit with candles on the tables and they sat in a corner booth which was a very romantic setting. A piano player played romantic melodies across the room and they laughed holding hands. The food and wine were excellent with Larry ordering her favorite food followed by a special desert accompanied by a crystal bud vase with a single red rose. After the desert was served, the waiter brought over a bottle of champagne and he poured some into two crystal flutes. Alex was wondering what this special occasion was, when Larry started to talk.

He looked into Alex's eyes and said, "Alex, I admire you for your accomplishments and hard work. You are beautiful both inside and out. You have made me happier than I have ever been and I would like to spend the rest of my life with you." He then handed her a small square box and when Alex saw the engagement ring in the box, Larry stood up, got down on one knee and proposed, "Will you marry me?"

Alex cried and between her tears replied, "Yes." The other patrons in the restaurant turned and said congratulations to them. Returning to Larry's place that evening, Alex felt closer and more in love with Larry than she could believe possible.

Even with their grueling work schedules, they still managed to spend almost every night together. Neither of their places was large enough for two persons, so Alex discussed the possibility of them getting another place and living together. It made sense to Alex with them being engaged but Larry said they would eventually but not right now. She didn't worry about their time apart when he played golf on Thursday afternoons and the times he met his coworkers for happy hour.

It was a rainy day in June when a Saturday morning surgery that Alex was supposed to do was cancelled. She kissed Larry who was still asleep when she left and it wasn't until she reached the hospital that she found out the surgery had been cancelled. She was delighted at being able to spend the day with him. When she left the hospital she did not call Larry since she thought that he might be still asleep and she could crawl back into bed with him. She was so excited to see him and tell him they had the day to be together, she hurried back, not even changing out of her scrubs. She picked up sweet rolls and joyfully went over to

Larry's apartment to surprise him. His car was there and she let herself in. He wasn't in his living room and she walked to the bedroom now thinking that breakfast in bed was what the doctor ordered.

Alex remembered every detail of that day too well.

When she opened the door to his bedroom, she saw Larry naked in bed having sex with his legal assistant. The shock of what she was seeing took a few moments to register and when it did, she couldn't say anything. They turned to look at her while they hurriedly tried to pull a sheet over themselves and without thinking, Alex threw the rolls she was holding at them and ran out.

A flood of tears came by the time she got to her car and her mind was racing with a barrage of thoughts and questions. Larry, whom she loved beyond reason, had lied to her and was he lying about loving her and wanting to marry her? He had bought her an engagement ring, by now she and proposed marriage to her. She was devastated and confused, wondering how he could do this and how long had he been unfaithful? She started to think about the social time he spent after work with the coworkers at his office. Was that time more social than she thought?

THE BOXES

Her world was shattered. Larry and her profession were her life. She had loved him unconditionally, and tried to understand what happened. She even wondered if he was one of those sociopathic people who were incapable of being in love. He couldn't love her and have done something like this.

One small part was that she was thankful that they were not living together. Did that make the breakup easier? There was nothing easy about this. She now questioned if that is why he didn't want to live together which made it easier for him to be unfaithful.

This infidelity did not just happen and Alex had not been gone long when she went to the hospital. A legal assistant just does not come over to his place early Saturday morning when she should have known that Larry was in a serious relationship. After all, Alex and Larry were always together at his company functions and Alex was wearing an engagement ring. Alex now questioned how long had this affair, friendship or whatever it was, been going on. Even worse, could there have been other women as well?

Her mind was racing and she wondered if she was that ignorant and did not pick up any clues. Was Larry that skilled a liar to hide this infidelity by telling her what she wanted to hear? She didn't understand as they were so close, talking all the time and they never even had a fight.

Driving away, all of these questions kept repeating in her mind and a part of her wanted to know the answers and yet the other part did not. She had to convince herself that this was over even though she felt like this loss left a wide gaping hole in her life and her heart. With all of this emotional turmoil, she called one of her fellow residents and asked him to cover for her for a few days because she was not feeling well. Saying that she was not feeling well did not even approach how badly she felt. Of course she knew it would take more than a few days for her to feel better but at least she had her profession, which was now her whole life.

The first night after the breakup with Larry was terrible for Alex as she was not used to sleeping alone so she slept little. She kept thinking that during the years that she and Larry were together, she believed she knew him completely and never imagined that he could do something like this. She was wronged and her pain now became anger at herself for believing and trusting him. She felt emotionally stripped, betrayed, and resolved that she would never trust any man again.

THE BOXES

Alex had too much time being confined to her hospital bed which made her remember her past even when she had tried to forget it.

After this horrible betrayal, somehow Sal materialized in her life. She tried not to think about that now as she was recovering in the hospital after her injury. She tried to sleep but got little thanks to the nurse's frequent checks on her.

THE BOXES

CHAPTER 6

LIVIA HISTORY

The weather in Arizona was clear and warm with little humidity. The vegetation around her vacation house was lush and green but Livi did not notice. It was a quiet town where the restaurants closed early but the sunsets were spectacular. Livi was often bored and ready to return home where she knew more people with whom to spend time. Ben was there and she didn't care that he was now married as she believed it would not last. Long ago she had met Ben at some clubs where she danced with him often but she couldn't understand why he wouldn't date her. Ben was a nice guy and they became friends, talking on occasion.

Livi was very attractive when she was younger, slim, with straight, medium length platinum blonde hair but her looks had been ravaged by time. Now her weight fluctuated from being very heavy to moderately overweight. She had thick legs and a large protuberant abdomen which she poorly hid by her bad choice of clothing. Instead of wearing loose dresses which would have looked better, she wore tight clothing, still picturing herself as being slim. Her hair was thinning but she kept the same hairstyle thinking it made her more attractive. She still thought of herself as a great beauty whom any man found irresistible. It didn't matter that the men she knew often avoided her and she didn't find a problem giving her phone number to her friend's boyfriends or dates.

Livi was jealous of her friends that accepted her and always criticized them, perhaps to make herself feel better. She did not understand why some friends eventually stopped being her friend.

Livi was a bitter person after her wealthy husband lost most of what he had through poor investments and she received only a small part of what of the wealth she should have inherited from her mother when she died. Unfortunately, in addition to the loss through investments, he was a gambler and lavishly spent what they had left. Her inheritance from her mother was in a trust that her husband couldn't access so Livi was left with enough money to have a comfortable life but not the lavish lifestyle she expected.

She spent a good deal of time alone but at least she talked to Ben, although not as frequently as she liked because of his marriage and he was too busy to have the lengthy conversations that she looked forward to. Their conversations always got around to him talking about Beth and Livi was tired of hearing about her.

In the past Livi's neighbors had invited her to dinner or social functions, but it was infrequent and she didn't understand why they had such little contact with her. They didn't understand why she never had any visitors. Livi was as affectionate a mother as she was able but substituted monetary help for affection and attention. Livi often talked about her past life and all of the homes that she owned in luxurious places. When she was not invited to the social functions she didn't care feeling it was her neighbors' loss. They actually got tired of her talking about herself wanting adulation from them.

Livi never gave her daughter any encouragement and spent little time with her or her friends while they were young even though she had the time. When her daughter was older, Livi started trying to spend more time with her as she had few friends. Unfortunately she was not a loving mother when Chloe, her daughter, was growing up and she was tired of supporting her lifestyle. Chloe had a lot of physical and emotional problems which prevented her from sustaining any real relationships.

Chloe knew of her mother's obsession with Ben because she talked about him often and was hoping he would visit or spend time with her. Chloe laughed at a joke she heard that people spend their lives trying to overcome their childhood and she felt that Livi was only her mother by birth. Chloe put herself through college and graduate school due to her mother's refusal to provide much financial support. This made her feel proud of what she had accomplished which her mother never acknowledged.

After Ben introduced Livi to Beth, she befriended her especially when Beth became part of their social circle. Livi started criticizing Beth just as she had done with his previous girlfriends. Livi was instrumental in Ben breaking up with them and still did not understand why he didn't want to be with her.

Livi had so much to be grateful for but she became a hard and opinionated person. She had few female friends and she discarded the ones she no longer needed. Many of her other friends started avoiding her due to her criticizing them and speaking badly of them to others. Fortunately she had Ben and she often complemented him trying to keep him endeared to her. She danced with Ben any time he would let her and she made certain she appeared with him in photos.

Ben told Livi everything about his girlfriends and even intimate details. Somehow she was able to convince him that they were not right for him. He completely missed how Livi would say or do anything or even lie to make him become disillusioned with every girlfriend, and his relationships did not last long. Ben never realized Livi's motive which was her belief that the only woman for him was herself. She waited for him to realize that.

When Livi was with Ben and Beth and saw the affection between them, holding hands, kissing, this inflamed her although she carefully hid her reaction. Her attitude towards Beth changed although she still feigned friendship with her. She started relating to Beth some terrible untrue things about Ben. She described him as being not smart enough, uneducated, a womanizer, and too low class for her. Spending time with Beth made it easier to tell these lies as she felt justified believing that Beth was wrong for him. Ben did not pay credence to what Livi said about Beth thinking they were just her rantings. Ben's relationship with Beth developed into a close and loving one and eventually marriage. This infuriated Livi and she started plotting their breakup.

After a year and a half of marriage, Livi continued to say deprecatory remarks to Ben about Beth, citing her being unfaithful and spending time with a successful Neurosurgeon. Ben did not have a formal education which Livi often mentioned which made him insecure. She even said that Beth complained about what he lacked. Ben trusted Livi and believed she was trying to protect him from being hurt.

Livi even tried to befriend Alex and arranged a lunch for them to talk. She related many horrible lies about Beth and then she meanly criticized Alex, even mentioning her makeup and the way she dressed. Alex was thin and pretty unlike Livi who was very overweight at the time. Alex realized that Livi was very jealous of her and Beth. Alex ascertained how mean she was and stopped talking to her. She did not relate to Beth what Livi had said because she did not want to hurt her.

After many conversations with Livi, Ben was confused and started believing her lies, even starting to question his relationship with Beth. Livi knew the time was right to introduce him to her friend, Marsha, extolling her praises and telling him she was the perfect woman for him. Marsha was attractive and a good dancer, which Ben liked. Of course Livi told Marsha that Ben was estranged from his wife and planning a divorce. This scenario was perfect for Livi and she believed that once she got him away from Beth, it would be easy to get rid of Marsha. Ben had never been unfaithful to Beth or any of his girlfriends, but he was convinced that his marriage was over. He was a decent man. Livi was elated when Ben started spending time with Marsha.

Beth's accident happened at the worst time for Livi and Ben realized that Beth needed him. He was going to help her so he was pulling away from Marsha to be with his wife. Livi knew that Ben would have inherited Beth's fortune if Beth had died in the accident and that she and Ben could have a wonderful life together. She now had no choice but to get rid of Beth and started thinking about ways to accomplish that. In her aberrant thinking, she felt justified in doing anything to be with Ben. She went back to her daily activities, plotting what she should do.

THE BOXES

CHAPTER 7

BETH ICU

The intensive care unit was very busy with the constant movement of the nurses taking care of the patients. The cardiac monitors beeped and there was the repetitive blowing of the respirators which was standard for any intensive care unit. The doctors were in and out, giving directions to the nurses and there were family members coming in for brief visits. Each patient was in a separate room with a lot of space for the nurses to work on them, although the patients were all visible from the nurse's station. It was a well-run intensive care unit.

Beth was awake and in pain which seemed everywhere although it was worse in one arm and one leg. Her memory of what happened was cloudy and she remembered only segments of what had happened. She looked around and found herself in a white room with tubes and bandages, machines beeping and her nurse checking on her often.

THE BOXES

Her nurse said, "Hi. I am glad to see you are awake and I am your nurse Leslie. It is Monday and you are in the intensive care unit. You just came out of surgery and how are you feeling?"

Beth's vision was still somewhat blurred it took a brief time for her to realize where she was. She answered, "Ok." even though she was not sure.

Beth tried to move and the pain was excruciating. She said "Ouch", but that did not adequately describe the pain she was feeling. Her left leg was wrapped in bandages with a splint elevated by a large metal sling and her right arm and hand were bandaged along with her abdomen. There was also a bandage around her head.

Beth said, "I am fuzzy and I can't remember much. What happened?"

Leslie replied, "You were hit by a car and were unconscious. You were in surgery for a long time but I am glad you are back. Your doctor has been in to check on you a few times and he will be back soon so he can answer your questions.

Beth's memory was starring to return and she thought about Alex. She asked, "What happened to my friend Alex and is she all right?"

Leslie answered, "She called a few times and you can call her. She is in the hospital for observation from a concussion."

Beth was relieved that Alex was alright and recalled how Alex had pulled her out of the way of a car on the street. She did not remember what happened after that. It must have been pretty severe for her to end up bandaged and her leg suspended. She thought about Ben and asked "Has my husband been by?"

Leslie replied, "He has been here most of the time and in fact he is in the waiting room now. Now that you are awake I can bring him in to see you but it can only be a very brief visit."

Beth was happy, "Yes I would like to see him."

Although Beth's memory was fuzzy she now recalled both cars coming at her and Alex and became very agitated.

 She tried to calm down before Ben came in. Ben entered the room and was shocked at Beth's appearance even though had been told by her doctors about the extent of her injuries. It was different seeing her with all of the bandages and her leg suspended. He was upset and angry at the same time, trying to understand how this had happened. He was upset that they could not reach him right away because he did not answer his phone when he was with Marsha.

He walked over to her and said, "How are you doing baby and are you in pain?"

"I have felt better." And she tried to smile. Even that hurt.

He expressed his concern, "Don't worry. I am here for you. I was so worried and when you get out of here I will be with you for anything you need." Beth heard what he said and was hoping he really meant it.

 Ben continued, "I love you and don't worry. You will be all right."

Beth was elated that he was with her and said to him, "I love you." and she started dozing off.

The nurse was close by and told Ben, "It's time to go as she needs her rest. You can see her later today."

Ben left the room and a flood of emotions overwhelmed him. Beth was badly injured and he had been with Marsha when it happened. Because of that he didn't find out about what happened until much later that day, he felt very guilty. Whatever Beth was alleged to have done didn't matter because she needed him now.

THE BOXES

Livi called Ben as he was leaving the hospital and still related terrible things about Beth. This made Ben was angry as this was the wrong time for Livi to say anything so callous. Nothing else mattered except Beth getting better. He believed her lies at the time when he started spending a sometime with Marsha and but he now wondered what kind of person demanded a lot of time be spent with her knowing he was married. If only he had not been with her when the accident happened, he could have come right away and Beth would not have been alone when she came to the hospital. Ben felt horribly guilty and Marsha did not seem to care when he finally got the message about Beth's injury. He recalled that Marsha never said she was sorry about what happened to Beth which made him realize how selfish and self-centered she was.

Ben had talked to Livi after he heard what happened and she did not seem concerned about Beth even though she said insincerely that she was sorry. She and Beth had been friends but Livi inexplicably stopped talking to Beth for reasons he did not understand. He knew that she and Marsha chatted like good friends and Livi often said that she and Ben made a perfect couple. He even asked her to call Beth and check on her and Livi said she would but she never did. Ben told Livi, "Beth was severely injured and I feel so guilty for not being around." He had

A change of heart about Beth and he continued, "She has no one but me and Alex and she will need a lot of help which I will provide for her."

Livi was unhappy at this change in Ben and unable to think of what to say, but finally asked, "What about Marsha? Beth's care will take up a good deal of your time as does your work. Don't forget that she did not think of you or me when she did all of those horrible things and what about her boyfriend?"

Ben was surprised that Livi could say that and replied, "I never found any proof that she had a boyfriend and you talked at length about the horrible things she did to you, but did she really hurt you besides your feelings? Why didn't you talk to her about those things before you trashed your friendship with her? Aren't true friends supposed to forgive and forget? I just don't understand."

Livi did not elaborate and did not comment about Ben's guilt and concern. Livi finally said insincerely, "Is there anything I can do to help? Call me if you need me or just want to talk."

THE BOXES

Ben thought about Livi's offer and responded, "I will, thanks."

Livi was beside herself and could not stop questioning why Beth was severely injured but unfortunately didn't get killed? That would have been so much easier for her, ignoring how that would have affected Ben. He often let Livi influence him even though she did it insidiously and it was so easy for her to convince him of things using facts that were lies. Ben wanted to take care of Beth now and this was a terrible turn of events for Livi. She tried to think of ways to get Ben back to her.

Chapter 8

Alex in Hospital-Meeting Sal

Alex awakened in her hospital room and didn't know what time it was but she had dosed off however briefly after her last neurological check by her nurse. Perhaps it was the effects of the concussion or her sleep deprivation that turned her thoughts to Sal. He helped her feel better about herself which she needed after being devastated by her former fiancé.

She had to stay in the hospital for another day or two for observation which she would have done with any patient given the severity of her injury and her symptoms.

Alex was happy and relieved that she had called Pete and was looking forward to seeing him, knowing that he could help find out what had happened. She wasn't sure that Beth would want to know what was going on but Alex certainly did, and in the back of her mind she wondered if the accident had anything to do with Ben. Dismissing this thought, she knew that he would never do anything to hurt

Beth even though his activities and change towards Beth did not make sense. She knew that Ben had strong opinions about things that Beth could not contradict but he also was a gentle caring man. Beth said Ben told her about his other female friends but he had assured her they were only friends.

The day was uneventful, although she was rescued by her friends who brought food and some diversions from the bleak boredom.

Later that evening, Alex was awake and with little else do and her mind wandered recalling her past. She tried to dismiss her thoughts of Sal whom she met years before, even though he would always have a piece of her heart. Sal was another loving and caring person as well as being a good husband and father. Most of the time Alex could justify their relationship, or maybe a love affair, but he still loved his family deeply and she did not take that away from him and never would.

Alex was starting the second year of her residency and grateful that her mentor Sean took care of his residents. He often invited them to the charity functions he attended because knew his residents could not afford nice restaurants and the food at these functions was spectacular. He was a thoughtful man. There was one particular function that Alex was looking forward to attending, that was in the elegant ballroom at a five star hotel where the buffet had fabulous food

Alex entered the ballroom thinking she did not mind getting dressed up for a free meal and especially for wonderful food. She had very little free time or at least she made sure she didn't, and definitely not enough to have a social life. She didn't want any involvement that started as a euphoric relationship but ended up in emotional upheavals.

Sean had also become a good friend and knew about her breakup but he never questioned what happened. He saw how it affected her and he never mentioned it understanding that she would tell him if she wanted him to know. Alex had been careful to keep her past as just that, the past. Alex was one of the best residents Sean ever had and as nice as person as he had ever met. He was angry that anyone could have hurt her like this. Money was tight for her as residents were paid little, but it was not as bad for the other residents who were married and had two incomes. He could tell that she was pale and quieter than before and did not laugh much, but she hid it well from everyone else.

THE BOXES

So Sean made sure he invited her to every social function where there was a lot of good food and lively surroundings.

Alex was on the slim side with an attractive, hourglass figure and never worried about what she ate even though she tried to have a healthy diet. Sean never intruded on her privacy when men were interested in her and she showed no interest. He also knew that her budget was tight with her having some school loans to repay.

Sean knew that Alex had lost her parents and did not have family for emotional support. She was bright and worked tirelessly without complaining, with diagnostic and surgical skills that were remarkable. She is cute too he thought and he smiled thinking that inviting her to these functions helped her out. When she arrived at the party, Sean was talking to some of the people he knew but he nodded to her. Getting a good meal was good for Alex as he figured she frequently missed meals being too busy to take the time and to save money.

Alex walked around the room chatting briefly but respectfully to some of the guests and thanked the hostess who smiled and was very gracious to her. Alex was wearing a simple fitted red silk dress and moderate heels with her thick chestnut hair falling in waves past her shoulders. She had even features with her sea green eyes and she never noticed the reaction that her striking beauty elicited. The hostess was wearing many large pieces of expensive jewelry and was older but it was difficult to know how much due to the procedures she had to hold back time. The hostess was pleased to have Alex there as she was a refreshing change from the rest of the patrons.

Alex still pictured herself as the skinny plain tomboy who was a science nerd and she was ignorant of the stares plus the hesitations in the conversations as she walked past the guests there. She appeared to be aloof but it was her inherent shyness and she did not engage in conversations easily.

Alex looked around and saw the elegantly dressed people, talking and laughing but she was quiet believing she could not add any merriment to the people there. She worked her way through the crowd to the buffet table to get some of the wonderful food which seemed to be in unlimited quantity. She was standing on one side of the room under a glorious chandelier and enjoying the salmon and caviar when she felt someone was staring at her. When she looked up she noticed a well-dressed man staring at her from across the room who was talking to Sean and they seemed to be friends. She dismissed this man's attention and went back to her food, trying to decide what she wanted to eat after this. But every time she looked up, no matter where she was standing, he was looking at her.

It did not matter to her because she had no intention of getting involved again and especially after her painfully failed relationship that left her believing that she could never have a normal loving relationship with anyone. Alex was more social in the past but now she did not feel like engaging in any lengthy conversations. Alex smiled to herself thinking that the standards of the patrons required high income or net worth but being a doctor, although a poor one, gave her a special dispensation for being accepted into a circle she had no interest in joining.

Sal had walked into the crowded ballroom and observed the ornate decorations with light from shimmering crystal chandeliers and an array of white candles in every corner. He noticed that this lighting gave a festive atmosphere for the many guests and sponsors of this charitable dinner which was for some chronic disease that he could not recall. There were too many of these functions to keep track of them but he was always invited as he contributed generously to these causes. These were causes like save the dolphins, whales, or starving children in countries of which he had never heard or anything to make the bored society wives and matrons honored for their time and monetary contributions.

These women had many thousands of dollars' worth of plastic surgery, designer dresses, and ornate jewelry and they believed that they looked good. Fortunately they were aided in their appearance by the dim light. They rarely worked for the money they pledged and they relied on their wealthy spouses or trust funds for their financial accolades. While they were busy with the charities their children were being raised by various employees such as housekeepers and nannies. Complaints about these alternate mothers were frequently the subject of lunches after shopping or tennis with the 'girls'.

A number of people attending recognized Sal and he knew that his contributions seemed to be all that he needed to make him look like an upstanding member of the community. He was grateful for his life place now as he was wealthy and respected which was a long way from his poor start in the Italian area in New York. It didn't take long before he was tired of the flashy bejeweled matrons of the moneyed social set coming up to him to thank him.

It was then that Sal noticed Alex, who was a breath of fresh air and wearing a simple yet elegant dress that showed off her perfect figure, wearing little jewelry and makeup. Unable to take his eyes off of her he thought that it was unnecessary to guild this lily. She had large breasts for such a slight frame with a narrow waist which he thought made her look very sexy. He never paid much attention to the women that attended these functions but Alex was different and he quickly observed that there was no ring on her telling finger.

Alex carried herself with her head held high and had a pleasant smile on her face like one seen on politicians talking to their constituents. She smiled to make her appear pleasant but it did not reflect happiness. It was far from obvious but Sal was very astute and detected a sadness that Alex had hidden from almost everyone that made her distant from her surroundings. He could tell that she was going through the motions of being social but nothing further.

Sal leaned over and was talking to the two large rough appearing men in dark tuxedos who came with him and stood by him at this event. He joked about the massive centerpieces with a multitude of multicolored flowers that were shaped like giant lollipops with a narrow glass base, wondering how the planners of these events thought of such things. The extensive table of food ran down the entire wall of the ballroom with every conceivable type of delicacy. It made him chuckle thinking that this much food could feed the starving people in one of the countries these functions were sometimes concerned about. He mentioned to his companions that they may as well have some food.

Sal put some food on his plate and felt like an outside observer who doesn't take any of this seriously but at least the food was very tasty although not as good as his mother's meatballs.

He talked to some patrons and his companions but he became silent when he looked at Alex as she walked around the room and noticed that she was there without an escort. He chided himself and questioned why should he care about one lady, and she was that, when there were so many attractive women that he knew. He was pleased that she was not with anyone.

Alex was now at the buffet table with her back to him and he could easily tell it was her from her long hair and slim but yet curvy figure. She flipped her hair back which was unfettered and moved naturally, unlike the coifs of the other women there. These other women there were dressed to impress the other patrons with their wealth which Sal did not find attractive and he thought that the jewelry was to perhaps make people not notice that they were aged.

Sal couldn't take his eyes off of Alex who occasionally looked in his direction, somewhat sensing that he was staring at her. Perhaps out of curiosity or boredom, Sal walked over to stand next to her at the buffet but he found himself looking at her fair face and high cheekbones instead of the food. She looked even more sensuous close up and he found himself speechless which never happened to him before. Alex acknowledged that he was there but she appeared to not to pay attention to him as she was more interested in the food.

He guessed that she was in her twenties and noticed that she was only wearing a small inexpensive watch, small silver earrings and of course no wedding ring. She was distant and he realized that meeting her was going to be tougher than he thought.

Returning to stand with his companions, he turned to one, pointed at Alex, and said, "Bruno, do you see that?"

"OK so it's a lady at the buffet. So what?"

Alex walked right by them with a plate of food and Sal again questioned his companions, "Look again and tell me what do you think now?"

Bruno looked at Alex up and down and spoke, "Very pretty but I like women a little more....dirty with huge breasts, although she does pass on that point. The rest of the dames here look scary and hard enough to hurt you."

Sal laughed a hearty laugh. "Thank you for your opinion and actually I have seen some of the women that you have been with and I know your type." He entertained himself with that remark.

Sal turned to Bruno "Go up to her and tell her I want to meet her."

Bruno said, "I have never seen you not just walk up to a broad. I guess this one must be different, but no problem boss." He walked over to Alex and he was just about to introduce himself when she turned around to face him. He was mesmerized when she looked up at him with her green eyes that were upwardly slanted and made he look exotic. Remembering why he was there he said, "Excuse me miss. There is someone here who wants to meet you."

THE BOXES

Alex was finishing some of the food delicacies she hadn't seen since the buffet at the last function when she heard Bruno speak to her. She turned around to see a very tall and muscular person whose size could fill a doorway. He had a gentle demeanor towards her so she was not intimidated by his sheer mass or even when he looked down at her and said, "Come with me."

Alex tried to chew quickly so that she could decline but he already had a gentle grip on her elbow so that she could not escape. Trying to pull away would have drawn attention to them and she preferred not to be noticed. She furtively looking around but there was no one to help her disengage. Before she could find a way to get away, another man walked over who greeted the large man and introduced himself as Sal. She looked up at the man who had been staring at her all evening and who was at the buffet table when she was there.

Sal was standing in front of Alex and thought to himself that she was even more beautiful close up. He noticed her fair, translucent skin and her full sensuous lips. Her eyes were a deep sea green color that he had never seen before. He was surprised that she was shy and did not realize how very attractive she was.

THE BOXES

Alex now looked up at Sal who was well dressed with dark hair and eyes. He was tall and well-muscled but not as massive as his friend. She was attracted to fit men who were muscular just like him, but when she looked at Sal who was looking directly at her, the attraction was immediate like a bolt of lightning. They started talked about meaningless things while looking into each other's eyes and Alex could tell he felt that the attraction was mutual. After a while he said, "You are a very attractive lady and I would like to spend some time with you. I am married and am not changing that."

Alex was stunned and didn't say anything. He told her he was married but the attraction was so mesmerizing that she didn't care. What was she thinking? This was light years away from anything she learned from her upbringing or from any of her moral and ethical standards, but it didn't matter.

Alex and Sal talked a long time and laughed often and although they never discussed the work that they did or their family, they never ran out of things to talk about. They talked about hopes and aspirations and both wanting to be happy and content with their lives. They looked into each other's eyes and Alex felt a very close connection which she had not felt since she had been with her fiancé. After her devastating experience with Larry, she believed that something was missing in her and she could never trust anyone to be involved again. This made her somewhat reckless and she thought that it did not matter what she did, as it would never work out anyway.

Sal felt a real connection to Alex with a strong mental and physical attraction even though they were together for what felt like only brief minutes. Alex had not enjoyed herself like this in a very long time and somehow this did more for her to erase the past than anything had.

Sal put his hand on her elbow and she felt a heady warmth and attraction with neither one noticing anyone else in the room.

Bruno and Marco, Sal's companions and bodyguards observed the interaction between Sal and Alex and Bruno turned to his companion commenting, "I ain't never seen the boss so interested in a broad but I guess nothing should surprise me."

Marco commented, "Same here but this one is different. Oh well, I am happy for whatever makes the boss happy and I guess he knows what he is doing." They smiled at each other.

Alex looked up and noticed that the crowd at the function was starting to thin out, with no idea how long they had been talking. Sal was also surprised and turned to Alex, "Can I walk you to your car?" Alex nodded. Sal walked over to one of the floral centerpieces, pulled out a red rose, and brought it to Alex which made her smile, especially when Sal brought her hand to his lips and lightly kissed it. They walked out together and Sal asked, "Do you need a ride home?"

Alex replied, "My car is here." not taking her gaze off of him.

As Alex was about to get into her car, Sal pulled her to him and kissed her for a long time. They lingered for a while and he asked, "How far away do you live?"

Alex told him and he knew it was in very modest area on the other side of the city.

Sal offered, "Let us follow you home to make sure you get there safely." Bruno and Marco were close as they always were.

Alex answered, "That's ok. I will be fine." Sal still had his arm around her, and she did not try to pull away still feeling the substantial mutual attraction between them.

THE BOXES

Sal was reluctant to let her leave and was not ready to be separated from her yet, so he mentioned, "I have a boat very close to here. Would you like to see it?"

Alex was looking into his eyes and without hesitation found herself saying "Sure." She couldn't believe that she agreed to go and her mind kept screaming 'what are you even thinking?' Alex was not thinking rationally as though she had no conscious choice and no free will here. Her attraction to him was overwhelming and she agreed to accompany him to the boat with one of his companions following in her car. Alex felt like this wasn't real and if it was a dream, she did not want to wake up.

Alex was in her hospital bed and felt a warm flush from her memory of meeting Sal and the happiness he brought her. She fell asleep with a smile on her face.

CHAPTER 9

ALEX DISCHARGE

The sun was already streaming in when Alex was awakened in her hospital bed by the nurse who came in to check her one last time. Alex smiled and tried to remember how many thirty minute naps she had between the hourly checks by the nurses. She gave up because sleep deprivation interfered with mental processes. There was a lot of activity in the corridor as usual but fortunately Alex was going to be discharged. It was a beautiful day, and she looked forward to going home and finally be able to get some sleep. She had a headache but she knew she wasn't allowed to be given any medication for that because of her concussion.

She was happy and relieved that she had called Pete and was looking forward to seeing him, knowing that he could help find out what had happened. She wasn't sure that Beth would want to know what was going on but Alex certainly did and in the back of her mind she wondered if the accident had anything to do with Ben. Dismissing this thought she knew that he would never do anything to hurt Beth, although his activities and change towards Beth did not make sense. She knew that Ben had strong opinions about things that Beth could not contradict but he also had a gentle, loving, caring heart. Beth said Ben told her about his other female friends but he had assured her they were only friends.

Alex dismissed her thoughts of Sal from the other night although he would always have a piece of her heart. Most of the time Alex could justify her relationship or maybe just a love affair with Sal although he said it did not change the love he had for his family. She did not take that away from him and never would.

Her doctor came to see her in the early afternoon, "I see you are already dressed so I guess that means I have to discharge you." They chuckled. "Do you have any questions?"

Alex replied, "Actually I have three pages of single spaced typed questions to ask you." They both laughed because they actually each had patients that did that.

"You can go home but you have to take it easy and no driving or I'll have to ground you."

"What do you mean ground me?"

"It works with my kids." They both laughed at his joke.

Alex called Mike to tell him she was being discharged but it could take up to several hours for the paperwork.

Mike was ready and said, "I will be there."

"I appreciate your taking me home. I am ready to sleep for a long time or at least for longer than 40 minutes." They both chuckled at this.

When Alex called, it did not take Mike long to get to the hospital which was just as Alex was signing the necessary papers for her discharge. Her nurse brought in a wheelchair.

Alex looked at the nurse and said, "You must be kidding. I can walk."

When Alex stood up she was a little unsteady at first, and Mike took her arm to support her. He said, "We did this before when I helped you out of the waiting room" and he smiled. He added, "You are on the other side now so act like a patient because you know that every patient has to be in a wheelchair to go to her waiting ride."

Alex assented, "I guess I could do worse, being under the care of a paramedic on the way home." She smiled at

Mike. It took a number of carts to bring all of her things to his truck, and she was grateful for his help. She had already received a number of calls offering help for going home and she felt very blessed.

Mike asked, "Will you be all right home alone?"

Alex replied, "Yes, that is what phones are for and I am not going to receive visitors yet. All I have are these few cuts and bruises."

Mike added, "And a concussion....."

They chatted pleasantly during the ride home which didn't take long as her home was fairly close to the hospital.

When Alex opened the door to her home, a flood of sunlight greeted her. Mike looked around and whistled to himself, thinking this was an elegant house with high vaulted ceilings and a lot of windows which allowed the sunlight to stream in. Mike noticed that the decorations were simple and tasteful but not flamboyant, realizing this was a comfortable place for her, a home and a refuge from the outside world. He could tell from her home, that despite her successful practice and her few friends she could be lonely. He believed that all that was missing in her life was someone to love and be with. He did not have a girlfriend and had not been with anyone in a while. His thoughts were drawn to Alex. He dismissed what he was thinking because she was obviously hiding from the world and was probably not ready for more than friendship with anyone. He couldn't think of anything more than that, but he was going to be a good friend to her while finding out about her life and her history.

Alex took her belongings into her bedroom and said, "Would you like some coffee and a snack?"

"That sounds great but let me help."

They ended up finding enough food for lunch and they sat on her sofa afterwards. The couches were cushy and comfortable which were more than decorative, like everything Mike could see. There was a large fireplace which would be warm and inviting when lit and even Alex's dishes were very tasteful, reflecting her refined taste.

Mike inquired after they had finished eating, "How are you feeling now?"

"Better now that I am away from the hospital and the food there."

Mike commented, "I guess the hospital food has a little way to go to achieve the status of a five star restaurant. On a more serious note, what are you thinking about the 'accident'?"

Alex thought for a few minutes before she answered reluctantly, "I don't know and I really don't want to talk about it. However, I am hiring a friend who is a private detective to find out what happened. He should be able to tell if it was an accident or if not and maybe find out who is behind it."

Mike tried to hide his frown when he mentioned, "Don't you think the police would do a good job finding out what happened?"

Alex replied, "They might be able to find out but sometimes I suspect they don't have the resources and time to investigate, especially since no one was killed. There are no suspects now as far as I know."

Mike was thinking and said, "It's not necessary for you to hire an investigator and what about the expense?"

"I am not worried about that because Beth is my best friend."

Mike offered, "Let me know what you find out and perhaps I can help or at least be supportive. Also, would you consider hanging out with a paramedic as a friend?"

THE BOXES

Alex looked at him and was actually pleased. And she liked the idea because he was the first person she even considered spending time with. She said, "I will think about that but now it is time for me to get some rest. The police already came by the hospital to talk to me and they are looking into it. Thank goodness they aren't going to bother me today for more information because I don't know what else I can tell them."

Mike helped her clean up and even put the dishes into the dishwasher. Alex gave him a tour of her house and he complemented her on much of what he saw. There were three boxes on the floor of one of her bedrooms upstairs and he asked, "What are these?" "They are just some mementos from the past." She explained.

"Everything else is put away. Do you need any help with these?" He thought this was a nice offer.

"I will get around to these sometime but thanks." She thanked him for the ride and he left.

Alex was happy to be home especially since it had been quite an ordeal and she was looking forward to some time by herself including some undisturbed sleep. She wasn't tired and looked at the four week stack of newspapers she hadn't had time to look at before. Alex still got the papers from her home town where she had been a resident, probably because every so often there was an article or an announcement about people she knew there including Sal and his projects. She knew it was ridiculous to get the paper but she did it anyway. She started with the oldest ones first and for some unknown reason she was drawn to the obituaries section, where she found Sal's obituary. She was surprised and hurt that Sal had passed away even though they had not had any contact for a long time. She felt that she had lost a very important part of her life and her heart, and she remembered the times that they were together. After all of this time she still cared and loved him. She couldn't contact his family for condolences because how could she explain her friendship with him to his family? They would not know who she was and they were never to know. He had a financial empire and she wondered about his successors and curious about the cause of his death. As close as they had been, she had no doubt that he had found another female diversion after her, since that was his lifestyle. She knew that she as well as his wife and children were kept at a distance about his businesses although she was certain he had provided well for them.

THE BOXES

Alex had her boxes of memories from their time together and why she kept everything which did not make sense to her except that it was like a fantasy that was wholly remote from her real life. The only one she could talk to about it was her old mentor Sean, but only about parts of her relationship. Sean was astute and he knew how much she and Sal meant to each other. She still kept in contact with Sean and they always made sure they took time talk or have a meal together at medical meetings.

Alex finally called Sean during lunch not wanting to interfere with the times he was seeing patients. He answered right away. Sean said, "I always like hearing from you but I admit that I was expecting your call. I guess you found out and I am sorry I did not call you because I did not want to be the one to tell you about Sal. It has been a while since we talked and how are you doing?" She related a little about her accident and that she was recovering from a concussion. He asked, "Are you alright and do you need anything? I am only a plane ride away. "Sean was a good friend and when they talked it was as though no time had passed.

"How did you hear about Sal?" Sean was a good friend to Alex and would have done anything to help her if she needed it. He was also a friend of Sal's. He knew that Alex was ready to move on despite how she felt for him. Even though he never talked about Alex, Sean knew how hurt Sal had been even though he had been expecting her departure. Sal, who talked to Sean a number of times after Alex had left and wanted to know how she was doing. His networks through his businesses could have kept track of her but he did not want to intrude on her except for what Sean told him.

"It was chance, or perhaps not, that I found his obituary although I suppose finding it happened for a reason. The obituary did not give any details and how did it happen?" She was having trouble accepting that he was really gone.

Sean replied, "They think he may have fallen off of his boat and drowned but they never found his body. There was a memorial service."

Alex was surprised because Sal was a good swimmer. Sean knew the world Sal was a part of and sometimes things happened. He did not relay his suspicions to Alex knowing that it was better that she not think about this.

Alex knew some things about Sal's extended family and his business associates but not everything. The explanation did not occur to her until she talked to Sean who was a little evasive about Sal's death and he was being careful with what he told her. She was still shocked about what happened and she could say very little.

Their conversation ended with pleasantries and Sean mentioned, "Come visit any time and I will see you at the conference next month, assuming you are better and can travel."

"You know that nothing can keep me down for long and before you say anything, I know I am not supposed to be driving." They both chuckled at her remarks.

"I forgot to tell you that two men came in asking about you and wanted to know how to find you. Of course I told them I had no idea."

"Thanks and it is had been good talking to you and catching up." Alex didn't think people looking for her was important even though she had been the mistress of the head of a large family syndicate.

When Alex graduated from her residency and had moved to a different state to start a practice, she began using her middle name Marsh as her last name to start fresh from her old associations. She might have been hard to find and perhaps that's why someone came to Sean's office to find her.

Sean added, "I didn't think anything about it and perhaps they were old patients even though I did not recognize them."

"I appreciate that but I am not going to worry about it." However she did not return to the newspapers and she started trying to watch some old movies on TV. She was sad and upset and didn't want to think about anything because Sal was still in a piece of her heart and always would be.

THE BOXES

CHAPTER 10

MEETING WITH PETE

Alex was finally able to get some sleep and she awakened to sun pouring into her bedroom. What a cheerful way to wake up because it was a sunny with the flowers and trees were blooming. It would have been a great day to walk around the lake behind her house, or be on a boat. In fact, she decided to do just that, take a walk around the lake and have coffee and a sweet roll at one of the little bistros by the water. Trying to keep herself from feeling guilty for some time off she justified it to herself thinking, 'I don't take enough time off for myself and it is time to smell the roses or whatever is blooming. I am not going to let myself feel decadent for eating a pastry or even two if I like. This is my day off and I can postpone the non-crucial errands I am supposed to be doing.' Alex was pleased with herself for taking some time off even though it was only a few hours and chuckling because she almost felt like she needed a doctor's note as an excuse. She smiled questioning needing an excuse for a sick day and why not a well day?

Alex was scheduled to see Pete that evening whom she trusted to find out what was going on with her and Beth. She had a feeling that she was not going to like what he was going to tell her. It was a beautiful day and she did not want to think about anything except feeding the ducks by the water. She blended in with the people enjoying the park by wearing jeans, a loose fitting tee shirt, sunglasses and her hair pulled back under a cap. The ducks were making a racket, pleased that they were being fed. After a while Alex noticed that that several well-dressed men seemed to be following and watching her while trying not to be noticed. She tried moving around the large pond at the park but they always seemed to appear close to where she was, although still far enough away for someone else who was not as observant as she to miss them. However, despite her concern she chuckled that they failed the inconspicuous part of keeping an eye on someone. While pretending to take pictures of the ducks Alex was able to get some distant photos of who she nicknamed the Yahoo's that were following her. Making fun of these men did not allay her concern that she was being watched and she knew she was seeing Pete later.

When Alex left the park she took a circuitous route home and checked her to see if she was still followed, but they were not in sight. She checked and did not see any suspicious cars around her house where she showered and changed to meet Pete.

Pete was very sharp and intuitive about people and he could tell right away when he met Alex, that she was a good person. Despite her being accomplished and successful he knew that she was a marshmallow inside, probably too nice. Alex did not hesitate to call him for his opinion about people and he always gave her good advice. They checked on each other on occasion which is what good friends do. Theirs was an eclectic relationship but they each knew they could count on the other for anything they needed, and she was grateful to have him as a friend. She met him years ago when he became her patient and another friend of hers hired him to help her in a sticky situation. Pete also helped Alex cope with her past about her breakup up with her fiancé several years before. They had no secrets from each other and she could confide in him about anything.

THE BOXES

They admired each other's outlook on life as well as their sense of humor and when they met for dinner it made for a mirthful evening. Pete liked Beth and was very concerned about her as well.

When Alex walked into the restaurant, she looked around because she had a very large practice and often ran into her patients, but she did not see anyone except Pete in a back booth. The patrons in the restaurant turned around to look at her as she passed by to sit with Pete and remarked to their companions how stunning she was. Alex never noticed as usual. She realized that it had been a while since she had seen him. He had not changed except that his hair was mostly white now and thinning. He was shorter than she with a rotund stomach and despite having to see some terrible things associated with his work as a private detective, he still had a cheery positive disposition. His wife had died of cancer a number of years back and although he had never fully recovered from his loss, he never talked about it. Every so often a sad shadow would come across his face which was fleeting and he quickly returned to his jovial self. Alex knew from their close friendship that he visited his wife's grave every day.

THE BOXES

Pete had a bachelors degree in criminal justice and had been a police detective in New York for many years. His marriage to his high school sweetheart lasted for over forty years and she was the love of his life. Unfortunately they were never able to have children but that did not change how much they loved each other. His wife lived four years after her breast cancer was diagnosed during which she had undergone multiple surgeries, chemotherapy treatments, and radiation therapy. Fortunately Pete was far enough in his career to be able to retire which gave him time to be with her through everything. He suffered with her and never left her side. Pete and his wife had become his nephew Chance's parents of sorts after his parents died and they were a close family.

Chance was now able to help Pete as he had helped him deal with his grief. It took a while for Pete to be able to carry on and try to decide what to do with his life, or what remained of it. He knew he wanted to help people and Chance suggested that Pete go into practice as a private detective. This appealed to Pete and he acquired a license to start his own agency. The work was rewarding and he felt that this was helping people in different ways than when he was a detective. What he was doing was challenging and interesting. He was able to help in situations like a wife worried about her husband having an affair or things like checking the veracity of employee applications for work. It was varied and interesting.

Sometimes Pete found more complex problems such as with investment or money, as well as marital issues. Pete was careful to not recommend couples therapy because that would have offended his clients and if they thought therapy would work, they would already have tried it. Unfortunately, it was his experience that marital therapy infrequently worked anyway. The degree of distrust and resentment had often progressed too far for them to listen to suggestions from a stranger who did not know them well. He believed that the only real chance at that point was for the couple themselves to realize that they really loved each other and could make compromises and changes to stay together. Marital discord was the majority of his business although, he did have a variety of other unusual but interesting cases. He did not like to call his clients cases as that made it sound impersonal.

It was interesting to Pete that large companies used professionals to do background checks on employees before they hired them, and yet people often went into relationships or marriages blindly while knowing very little about their new mate. He found an occasional man or woman who despite alleging that they were single, were still married and even still supporting a wife and sometimes children. He sometimes found a whole array of aliases, forged birth certificates to hide illegal aliens or criminal offenses with or without incarcerations.

It was so easy for a woman or man to just google the name of someone before they even dated or spent time together. Just looking someone up on google, Pete found lists of bankruptcies, felony convictions, and only alleged professionals like doctors or lawyers. He knew that just listing the name of an actual physician brings up a number of full pages on google showing previous and current practice locations. Checking on google was so simple but people did not even think of that.

Pete tried to forget the sad things he had seen where women had been taken for their life savings by a boyfriend or a husband they had not known long, and sometimes even after they had been together for many years. Despite all of his efforts, most of the perpetrators that took money could not be found and the ones that were found had no assets to recompense the poor victims. Pete had seen some evil in the world that no one should have seen both when he was a police detective and now that he was a private detective. He knew Chance had seen a lot as well and thinking it was just part of the job did not adequately release these memories.

Pete had a good heart and was happy to have Alex as a very close friend. He was entertained that when they met anywhere, she was so stunning that everyone turned around to look at her. He could tell they were thinking, what must he have to be with her? They both smiled when they made eye contact as Alex slid into the booth across from Pete.

Alex smiled and asked, "You look good Pete and how business is? We don't get together enough and it is a shame that it has to be under these circumstances."

Pete could tell that Alex was stressed but trying to hide her concern. He answered, Business is booming. "I agree and we should do this more often and especially in more pleasant times. I want you to know that I am unhappy that you and Beth were hit by a car and ended up in the hospital, but I am more upset that you did not call me right away." He chuckled and added, "Don't do it again! You are still as beautiful as ever, inside and out."

This made Alex smile, "I won't do it again Boss."

They talked for a while about mundane things, caught up about things in the past, and the good meals they had together. It was a light conversation.

Becoming more serious, Alex related the details of their accident, the injuries, and her conversations with Beth. Pete took notes which he always did and Alex joked with him, "Are Beth and I going to be a chapter in the book you write?" This lightened the mood a little.

"I hadn't planned on writing a book but if I did you and Beth would have a whole book of your own." They both chuckled.

Pete continued, "I don't know anything about when you were struck by a car and I wanted to ask you if it was ok to get some help from my nephew, Chance, who is a police detective. What you and I talk about is confidential as you know so I wanted your permission before I said anything."

"You have my permission and I trust anyone you do because more help is always welcome. And before I forget to tell you, several men may have been following me around the lake this morning when I was feeding the ducks. They were definitely too well dressed for the park and I clandestinely got their photos along with the ducks of course.”

"Maybe you are in the wrong business. “This made them both laugh. He told her, "Let me see the pictures and text them to me and I will see what I can find out about them."

Pete looked smiled at her and, asked, "How is your love life?"

Alex chuckled. "What love life?"

Pete commented, “If I was 30 years younger....." and they both smiled at each other.

When they finished eating, Pete pulled out a Manila folder. Pete was now serious and he looked at Alex, "I am going to tell you some things that are not good and I want to be sure that you are ok so shall I continue?"

Alex replied, "Doctors see a lot of bad stuff which doesn't make it easier but we have had practice coping with it. I want to know what you have found out.”

Pete started out, "I have not discovered anything about the car striking you, but I am afraid that Ben does have a girlfriend that he sees but never spends the night with her." He looked at Alex to see her reaction but she wasn't showing any emotion so he continued, "She is a sales person in the cosmetics department at an upscale department store and this lady, Marsha, has a fairly nice apartment and car which are unlikely that she can afford. She must be receiving some financial help from someone, although I could not tell from where. We can suspect that Ben may be helping her financially but we can't substantiate it, and she could still be receiving benefits from elsewhere."

Alex was still silent, not knowing what to say and realizing that the problems between Beth and Ben may have a reason. She wondered if Livi's rantings about Beth could have cast a shadow on their relationship. Beth did not express her concerns about someone else so this news would be devastating for her.

Pete pulled out the contents of the manila folder, "Here are the pictures and information. Her name is Marsha Gregson, thirty years old, never married and no children. Her father is a car mechanic and her mother a cashier at a supermarket."

Alex looked at the pictures showing her with Ben who had his arm around her. She was not really pretty, with long bleached blond hair, dark roots and a voluptuous figure which she showed off with tight fitting clothing and short skirts. The jewelry she wore was large fashion jewelry which Alex thought was flashy and tacky. It was difficult for Alex to believe that Ben could be interested in someone who looked so low class when he was married to Beth, who was very sophisticated and classy.

"Beth did not believe that Ben had an outside interest although she did wonder about it and was concerned about the little time he spent at home. She told his attitude towards her had changed from nice and caring to be always critical."

Pete was concerned and tried to hide it. "He did not try to hide his affair much and most likely he was seen with Marsha by some of their friends and acquaintances. Beth probably would have found out about the affair at some time, but sometimes friends don't relate what they have seen to the injured party. That is a shame because the longer it goes on, the more likely that person is hurt."

"I know that is a tough call as to whether to tell a friend about an indiscretion to prevent your friend from being blindsided, but sometimes if you do say something, you lose a friend." Pete nodded his head in agreement.

Alex saw the truth in the color photos but she was still surprised and shocked. She thought that Beth had suspected that Ben was seeing someone else, but there is one thing to suspect it and another to find out it was true. She had been certain Ben would never do that because he was a decent man and Alex always thought they were the perfect couple. Alex asked, "How often does he see her?"

"Almost every day, during the day or early evenings and sometimes they just go out to eat. Since Beth has been in the hospital he has been going over to Marsha's often." Pete showed her more photos.

Alex wondered if something had happened to Ben to cause him to do that, like Livi's lies and her close friendship to him. Alex did not know that Livi was carefully planning this and had introduced Ben to Marsha.

Pete continued," And Beth was definitely not seeing anyone else."

Alex was upset at the news about Ben because it was already heartbreaking for Beth with Ben distancing himself from her.

"I am never going to be able to tell her when she is stuck in the hospital and will be for a while. Hopefully she never needs to know. Ben is her whole life and she would be devastated. She has a way to go to get better so now is not a good time to upset her." Alex hoped Beth didn't hear about it.

Pete added, "There is something else."

"There is more? What other bad news do you have?"

Pete replied, "I will just have to say this. Ben is having financial problems with his businesses.

Alex said, "What? Oh no."

Pete and Alex looked at each other, thinking the same thing.

Alex blurted out, "Ben never cared about Beth's money because had his own and he could never harm anyone."

Pete added, "That was before but they are now living a very nice lifestyle, Ben has another friend of interest and for the first time his businesses are in trouble. If he and Beth got a divorce he wouldn't get anything since you told me that all of Beth's money is in her trust including the house."

Alex was silent, not knowing what to think. To change the subject, she asked," Did you find out anything about the accident?"

Pete replied, "I haven't been able to find out anything so far and whoever did it covered his or her tracks well. There is something else to consider. Do you know if you or

Beth were the target and do you or she have any enemies?
Can you think of anyone?"

Alex reflected, "Not that I know although there is now
some suspicion with Ben but I still don't believe he could
do anything like this. And I almost forgot to mention that
were two men looking for me, at my office, and at the
hospital but I was busy and they did not stick around to talk
to me. I have no idea who they were or what they wanted
and I did not think anything of that."

"I can try to check on them and do you have any idea
why what they wanted?" Pete was concerned.

"I have no idea. The girls said they were big,
muscular and didn't smile."

"We should check on all of these things. My nephew
can give a different perspective on what is going on with
his access to records that I don't. Actually he made an
appointment to see you as a patient for a minor medical
problem that you can help him with. We may as well keep
it in the family."

Alex commented, "I will keep these photos and your
notes assuming these are copies for me and Beth although I
am going to keep them from her right now. She cannot be

upset while she is getting better and Ben was and still is the love of her life. I won't do anything that could hurt her."

They talked some more about social things and Pete said he would let her know if he found out anything else. They hugged each other promising to keep contact more and they left.

CHAPTER 11

BOAT WITH SAL

That evening after meeting with Pete, Alex was upset at what he had told her. She had trouble sleeping and trying to distract herself. Her thoughts turned to Sal, remembering the details of the time she spent with him. She chuckled about the night she spent with Sal on his boat after meeting him for the first time. She remembered waking up on the boat with Sal the next morning.

Alex had slept well which was which was rare for being in the second year of her surgery residency that required many hours of work. Sleep was a luxury and she felt well rested but when she woke up she wasn't sure where she was. Her first thought was that she was late for making rounds on her hospital patients. As a resident she was responsible for seeing the patients but when she looked at Sal next to her, she realized she was on his 'boat' with him. How she got there and the events of the night before came back to her and she thought, what was I thinking? She smiled, mentally answering her own query acknowledging that rationale thinking had nothing to do with this. She now remembered that it was Saturday and she was not on call so the patients could be seen later.

Now that Alex had time, she started looking around the massive cabin she was in and realized that this not just a boat but a very luxurious yacht. The room was the size of a large hotel suite but much more elegantly decorated and the art alone looked like some pictures she had only seen in museums. She actually felt safe and secure in a way she had never felt and they made love again, languishing in each other's arms.

The night before they did not take the time to make a tour of the massive vessel but she did not care, because it was good just being with Sal whose confidence and sense of humor made her forget the past. The two glasses of wine that she drank was not enough alcohol to wipe out her reasoning ability but that didn't matter. She was ordinarily cautious but this was different and there was no justification for her to have come with him to the boat. She could have been abducted or murdered but she still went with Sal. He was incredibly attractive but she wondered, why now and especially with this married man.

THE BOXES

The night had been like a fantasy and not just about sex because they talked at length, laughed, he tickled her, they showered together, plus spent time in the hot tub. There was real communication both physically and mentally and they were truly connected, apart from the rest of the world. Alex could not remember ever being that close to anyone so quickly and even with her ex. She thought she had been very close to her ex but now realized that it was more like a causal relationship compared to this. There were no secrets now with Sal, although he never discussed his businesses or other relationships in the past. Yes he was married and loved his family, but he did explain that he usually had a girlfriend as well. Alex kept herself from asking anything about this and she knew that one of her problems was questioning things too much. He did volunteer that this ship was for his personal time with friends and not for use by his family because they had plenty of other things that kept them busy.

One of Sal's companions drove her car to the boat the night before when she rode in his large black sedan, thinking that it made her feel better to have her car here so that she could leave any time. She was happy and content just being here with Sal although she knew that soon she would have to return to her life as a resident.

Sal slept with his arm around Alex which made her feel safe from the world. She was looking at him, thinking he was a very nice and attractive man when he started to stir. He said, "Good morning beautiful. How did you sleep?"

She smiled at him realizing how disheveled she must look and replied, "Quite well, thanks, and you?"

"Good because I think I slept better than I can remember. You are a remarkable lady, smart funny, and very, very sexy. Meeting you last night, especially at one of those charity functions was meant to be."

Alex felt the same way but she did not want to admit it and said, "I bet you say that to all of the ladies you have just met and spent the night with."

He wasn't smiling when he said, "Is that what you think, that this is just a fling? I do not do that and there are plenty of ladies around for me to be with if I want but I do not bring them here. I don't think you realize how special you are and do you feel comfortable here?"

Alex thought that it was an unusual question, especially after they had spent a glorious night together.

This was beyond any expectations that she could have imagined and he was asking if she was comfortable? She had to hold her tongue to not say anything to allow him to clarify and replying only, "Yes, very much so."

He mentioned, "I am glad to hear that you feel comfortable here because you will be spending a good deal of time here with me." Alex thought that it was an interesting comment that she did not know how to process.

Alex looked around for her dress and when she did find it, she laughed at it being part of the mound of clothing next to the bed with both hers and his attire from the previous evening. The dress was a wrinkled mess and he chuckled at its condition. He gave her some shorts, a top and some sandals that fit her to wear. She wasn't about to ask whose they were or where them came from but that brought her around to reality.

While Sal was dressing, she said, "Sal, I have to leave to make rounds on patients because even Saturdays are work days for doctors." She didn't remember telling him that she was a doctor but it did not matter the night before.

"I am pleased you came here because last night was a very special night for me, with a remarkable lady." And he smiled a smile that made her melt.

Alex smiled also and she was thankful that she kept an extra scrub suit in her car to wear to the hospital in case she needed it, although she never had an occasion to use them until now. Her place was a long drive away and the hospital was now close saving her the necessity of going home to change before going to work.

When she was ready to leave, Sal stood in front of her holding his arms on her shoulders with his hands clasped around her neck and he asked, "Are you sure you cannot stay?"

Alex didn't say anything knowing she had to leave and wondering if he was serious about her coming to spend time with him because she could have been just a one night stand. If he was serious, she had a mixture of feelings of being pleased or concerned that he wanted her to spend a lot of time with him. He also just assumed that she would without asking her if that is what she wanted. She smiled at herself because that answered her question and if he wanted it, she was willing to see him often. There was no disagreement there.

Of course she did have a day job that took up much of her time and he would have to respect that. After all, her profession was her future and as wonderful as her time was with him, she believed it was temporary even though there was definitely no place else she wanted to be right now.

When Sal saw Alex at the charity function he was stunned by her striking beauty and grace.

He observed that Alex had class and breeding besides being beautiful, noticing that she did not know how stunning she was or how much attention she received from the patrons at the party. Despite her seeming to be aloof, he knew immediately that he wanted to meet her. He sensed a sadness in her as though something terrible must have happened but she hid it well. He was astute after his many dealings with people so he was able to discern it, even from a distance. Most or all of the other guests there would not notice as they were too self-absorbed. Now he wondered what he would have to do for her to consider spending time with him.

When they met he enjoyed their conversation but he knew very little about her when he invited her to his boat. Sal had a number of extramarital relationships in the past, but they did not last long and having girlfriends outside of marriage was normal for the group of people with whom he associated. Getting a divorce was never a consideration for any of them and he could tell that Alex was not the type to be involved with a married man.

Sal was never shy, although reserved but he smiled at his need to have one of his companions ask her to meet him. Sal was surprised but very pleased that she agreed to go with him to the boat. Once they were together, it was a good night beyond that which he had experienced and especially for someone so seemingly reserved, she was unrestrained in bed. She was really fun to be with outside of the incredible sex. They laughed and joked, talked about many things and she was a real joy to be with. She made no demands of him and seemed to accept the situation as it was. He felt a real connection to her, physically and mentally which had never happened to him in the past. His previous girlfriends were not very bright and were obsessed with how they looked the or material things that he could give them. This was the first time he felt that he met someone he respected who just wanted to spend time with him without asking for anything. Although Alex seemed happy when she was with him, he could sense the cloud of sadness around her. He was going to try to change that and he had never felt protective of any of his female friends before.

He felt a sense of loss when she left that day as he really liked her, and he was hoping that she would not get frightened and run from him. That had never happened with him with anyone he wanted to be with but she was different.

Alex left the boat in a dinghy to go ashore where she was taken in his limousine to her car. She looked back and muttered to herself, "I have totally lost my mind." She made it to the hospital and made rounds on her patients although her thoughts kept returning to Sal. He was kind and gentle with a good sense of humor. He was also so attractive that she had to keep putting him out of her mind to concentrate on what she was doing. She would definitely spend time with him again and worrying about the future did not matter as she was living in the present and enjoying it.

Waiting at the nurse's station at the hospital was a huge bouquet of flowers from Sal and the nurse at the desk there told her, "Lucky you and does he had a friend?" Alex wondered about how he knew where she worked because they never talked about it, maybe about everything else, but not about reality.

THE BOXES

It did not matter except that this made her feel good and she went back to work thinking, how could anything so good be bad but whatever happened she was having a great day.

CHAPTER 12

BETH IN HOSPITAL-DARK FIGURE

The evening was cool with heavy rain when Alex came to visit Beth who was still in the hospital. Alex was now back to work full time and feeling few repercussions from her injuries but unfortunately that was not the case for Beth. Her injuries had been very extensive and she was lucky to be alive. Driving up to the hospital reminded her of when they were injured but least the cars on the road had their headlights lit which made her chuckle, a nice change. This time she planned to take her umbrella out of her car and use it although the rain was only water and it was not going to make her melt like a wicked witch. She smiled thinking about all of the times she left her umbrella in the car. Why even have an umbrella if it is never used?

Alex still didn't know why she and Beth were injured and she kept running scenarios in her mind as to why it happened. She tried to think of any old grudges, fights, unresolved anger in anyone who knew either of both of them but she could not think of anyone or any situation.

She even wondered if there were any friends from grade school, high school, college or even work that wanted to harm them. This thinking was getting a little out of hand and she was tired of thinking about it. She was here at the hospital to see Beth and cheer her up.

Alex parked the car and very cautiously looked around for any moving vehicles or anyone suspicious walking around before she got out of the car. She was not supposed to be driving soon after her concussion but she did. She smiled knowing that doctors are the worst patients for following instructions, herself included.

Alex made sure she came to the hospital every day to see Beth and was pleased to see that Beth was in good spirits which would help her to heal. Alex talked to Beth's nurse often to follow her progress and now Beth was now in a regular room although she was still not allowed out of bed. Alex tried to cheer her up and she often succeeded but what made Beth the happiest was when Ben came to see her. He was there every day and although many of his visits were brief and every few days he stayed in Beth's room on a chair that unfolded into a bed. Beth even laughed when he joked that her leg suspended on the metal brace looked like a TV antenna. This made her think of the happy relationship they had in the past. She wondered if things were going to be better now between them.

Ben always called Beth when he was on the way to the hospital which pleased Beth because it gave her a chance to comb her hair and put on makeup. Alex's visits sometimes coincided with Ben's and she was pleased to see them happy together even if it took this accident to have this happen.

Alex could tell that Beth was feeling better now despite being confined to a hospital bed and exhibiting what Alex called, ' the positive makeup sign'. Alex had observed that when a female patient was feeling better she started wearing makeup again, assuming that she wore makeup before.

Alex performed her surgeries and admitted patients to the hospital where Beth was which made it easy for her to visit often, even if it was only for a few minutes. Being a doctor she not have to observe the limited time schedule for visitors.

Alex came in to Beth's room, happy that Beth was in good spirits and asked, "How is the patient today?" Beth smiled and Alex already knew the answer to her question because Ben had just left. The room was cheerful, with flowers, candy, plants and balloons everywhere, mostly from Ben.

Beth said, "I am always happy to see you and I am as good as a person can be under these circumstances." When she pointed to her casts and bandages she chuckled as did Alex. Beth finally asked for the first time, "Did the police find out anything about 'that night'?"

Alex replied, "Not really but I am not worried and you shouldn't be because your energy is best spent getting better. And before you ask, your vegetable garden is fine and one of your neighbors' son is enjoying taking care of it, especially since he is being well paid." They both laughed because Beth had not even thought of her garden until now.

Beth asked since Mike had visited her a few times, "What is with you and that tall, good looking fellow that comes to visit me?"

"You must mean Mike who was the paramedic that came to our aid the night we got hurt and he is just a friend."

"Ok, whatever you say." She smiled.

Alex and Beth chatted some more about ordinary things when Alex said, "Well, I have to get back to work since am not lucky enough to be able to lie around in bed all day." they laughed heartily and Alex left.

Alex was spending time with Mike although it was only occasionally. They were just were friends which was fine for Alex even though Mike wanted to spend a lot more time with her. She knew he was fond of her and although they often talked or texted, Alex was not interested in anything more or at least not now. Mike helped Alex with some chores around her house and she was glad he came to the hospital to visit Beth. Alex still did not trust any man even though Mike seemed very nice and caring. He had a busy schedule as she did, but they did find a little time to spend together and he even came to her house a few times for dinner.

Mike offered to help Alex with anything she needed and still offered to help her with the unpacked boxes he had noticed in one of her bedrooms. She declined repeating that she would go through them sometime. Alex still hadn't been able to think about or do anything with the boxes of things from when she was with Sal. And now she was mourning his death and thinking about him brought back a surge of memories even though they were in the distant past. He may have been the love of her life but she did not want to label her relationship with him like that. She knew she would look at the contents when she was ready.

The boxes had letters, photos and even some of the clothing she had worn while she had spent time with Sal. When Alex had moved out of her apartment she took some things to Beth's house including a few boxes and someone which were still there. She never thought about why she couldn't address the boxes but she wasn't ready to extricate that part of her past from her life.

Alex was writing notes on her patients at the nursing station when one of the nurses that Alex worked with, who was also a friend, mentioned that the two men that had been looking earlier that day but Alex was in surgery and they did not wait. Alex wondered if it was the same men from the lake. She was told the men were casually but well dressed and not very communicative. Alex didn't think about I'd because she had a lot to do and continued seeing her patients. She felt good that she had a busy practice which gave her less time to worry about what had happened.

Livi was still out of town but continued communicating with Ben as often as he let her, and she still told him ridiculous things about Beth. Ben was smart enough to know that Livi always made things sound worse. However, as often as he was told about Beth's affair and other details he started thinking that some of what she said could be true. He didn't know Livi was on a mission to discredit Beth with Ben.

When Ben came into Beth's room, sat down and took Beth's hand, Beth asked him, "Have you heard anything from Livi? She doesn't return my calls and the last time I even communicated with her was when I visited her a long time ago."

Ben did not know what to say because he heard from Livi often and she repeatedly talked about Beth. Ben felt that Livi was his friend and did not realize how much Livi was trying to manipulate him. He refused to tell Beth about the allegedly horrible things that Livi said she had done and were the reason that Livi stopped talking to her.

Livi called Ben a number of times and when he finally picked up, she asked, "How have you been doing?"

"Good. I am at the hospital and they don't know when Beth can come home."

"Are you still seeing that wonderful lady Marsha?" She didn't want to hear about Beth.

THE BOXES

"I am very rarely but she demands too much and where did she get the idea that I was divorcing Beth? I won't see her anyway when Beth comes home and I will be there for her." Ben still felt guilty that he was not around when Beth was injured and he realized how much he loved her.

Now Ben was back with Beth to help her and Livi felt it was not fair because Ben should be helping her, not Beth. Livi could not let this happen and had been working on a solution to get Beth out of Ben's life. Beth was interfering with their relationship and ruining her life. Did Beth even plan this accident to get him back? Beth loved him and would do anything for things to be as they were before. Livi was so upset and angry that she was not thinking rationally.

Beth was in the hospital for what would be a lengthy recovery and she was still pale with a lot of bruises but she was alive and getting better. Her doctor told her that eventually she would not have trouble walking from her leg injury which was a relief but she had a lot of rehabilitation to do. She was still in a lot of pain receiving a lot of medication through her IV which she knew was temporary.

Ben stayed a for a while after the nurse gave Beth a sleeping pill knowing that she was exhausted but happy that he was there to see her. They chatted pleasantly which cheered her up with him showing care and concern and talking about her returning home. What Beth did not know was that Ben was spending some evenings with Marsha who was thrilled to have him spend time with her. Ben was conflicted because he liked spending time with Marsha and the attention she gave him but he loved Beth who needed his help. Beth was happy and felt like things were changing for the better with Ben. He kissed her, waited for her to fall asleep, and left.

Neither Ben nor the nurse had seen the dark figure standing in the hall close to Beth's room. This man easily obtained It was easy for the man waiting in the hall to get a vial of medication and a syringe from the medication cart while the nurse was in another patient's room administering medication.

The dark figure looked around to see if anyone was looking and seeing no one, he slipped into Beth's room. He quickly opened the package containing the syringe and drew the liquid from the vial into it. This was almost too easy and the instructions he was given were perfect. He believed he was doing a good deed by getting rid of a very evil person.

THE BOXES

CHAPTER 13

HECTOR

Hector had only been in this country two years when he met Livi in a grocery store when they were comparing prices on some sale items. He was a medium height, average looking but fit man and they laughed and started joking about the store, which led to a long conversation over coffee. Hector was a handyman and started spending time with Livi including coming over to her house to help her fix a lot of things. While Livi and Beth were still talking, Livi recommended Hector's services as a handyman to Beth who also gave his name to Alex.

Hector lived in a very modest efficiency apartment and was always looking for work which was sparse. He shopped for Livi and even went with her while she was seeing doctors for one of her numerous medical problems. He was entertaining and took her mind off of Ben somewhat but not for long. Livi had acquired a lot medical knowledge from researching her medical problems and her visits to doctors.

Livi began spending a lot of time with Hector and he loved her deeply since she seemed to accept him as he was, a poor construction worker with no education.

Livi was restless however, and she told him how upset she was and how evil Beth was explaining that she had started seeing her husband while they were married. It was too easy for Livi to tell stories but she did what she had to do believing this was justified. Livi related, "Beth was jealous because we were happy and she started trying to be with my husband by fabricating excuses for him to help her with a lot of things. They ended up having an affair and she ruthlessly induced him to take all of our money out of our bank accounts and sell the house to her. Unfortunately all of this of was unknown to me and I only found this out when I was served with divorce papers. I knew my husband and I had some problems and disagreements but nothing that we could not work out. I now realize our problems had everything to do with her. He left to move in with her and fortunately, as was agreed in our divorce decree, I was given the right to continue to live in the house. She ended up with all of our money and I was left with very little. I would love to go back to work but I cannot can't because of the medical problems I have.

Hector believed Livi when she related this story to him and told him they subsequently divorced. Livi explained that her husband moved in with Beth before the divorce when he gave her almost everything. Just after the divorce, Livi said Beth threw him out when there was nothing left to get from him and he was left with nothing. Now Livi said Beth was her landlord and was trying everything to get her out by charging exorbitant rent, including refusing to make repairs. Livi said she expected to be evicted any time and she had no money to get another place.

Livi described Beth as a calculating monster and explained that there was nothing she could do because what Beth was doing was legal even if it was wrong.

"That was a horrible thing for her to do." Hector was concerned and sympathetic.

"This was really mean. My ex-husband is a broken man and I could never go back to him because he hurt me so badly. I could never trust him again."

Hector believed this story because he loved her and he hated so see her so upset and beside herself. Hector tried to console Livi and wanted to help her but he did not have any money and his very small place was too shabby for Livi to move there.

Hector had heard enough and he was enraged. He said, "In the country I came from, there are other ways to get justice." That is just what Livi hoped to hear and knew she had picked the right person to be involved with. Hector went on, "I do not know enough to take care of this but I will do anything to help."

Now Livi suggested that the only way she could protect herself was if Beth had a complication in the hospital. She was pleased that she had even convinced Hector that this was his idea. She was very manipulative and Hector had no way to determine the truth in Livi's story.

Livi was happy that maybe something could be done to bring Ben back to her. She related, "This has to look like an accident and let me think about how it can be done." She had to make certain that she was not involved except as an innocent bystander.

After watching some crime movies and some TV shows, Livi was able to figure out a way to get rid of Beth. She smiled at how much information was available about committing a crime. She was able to give Hector careful directions for him to accomplish this task.

She instructed Hector, "Dress in dark clothing for when you go to the hospital and wait in the hall outside of Beth's room until there is no one around. Then go to the medication cart when the nurses are in a room with a patient and won't see you. Get a syringe with a needle and a bottle of insulin. Do you understand that?" He nodded and she went on, "Next pull the liquid from the bottle into the syringe like I am showing you and stick the needle into the bag of liquid by her bed, injecting all of it. Make sure there is no one around to see you and then calmly walk away. This will simply look like she had a complication from her injury."

Unfortunately Hector had trouble remembering so Livi had to write out Beth's name and the spelling of insulin. She instructed him to get rid of the note so that there was no evidence just in case something went wrong.

Hector wasn't sure about taking a life but he saw how much Livi was upset and had been convinced that there was no other way to save her. He was resolved that he would do it for Livi whom he loved.

THE BOXES

Ben loved Beth and had been with her that evening at the hospital, talking and planning for the future. She was very happy when he was there and he stayed until she fell asleep. When he left he didn't notice the darkly clad figure standing in the hall.

Hector waited until Beth's visitor left and the hospital hallway by her room was clear. The nurse's medication cart was close and he easily found what he needed. He took the plastic wrapper off of the syringe and when he drew the liquid from the vial into the syringe, he injected it into her IV bag.

Livi told Hector that the drug would take a while to work so he had time to get away. He was ready to slip out of the room when he heard someone in the hall. He hid behind the door and waited knowing he could not be caught especially with the syringe. He looked around for a place to get rid of it quickly and decided to throw the syringe and the plastic covering into the trash basket next to the bed. He tried to cover them with trash in the basket so they would not be noticed. He didn't think to wear gloves when he did what he was instructed to do. The hall was now deserted again so he was able to leave without hurrying which might have attracted unwanted attention.

He called Livi on the way home, "Everything went well." He felt good that he had taken care of her and now she could be relieved so they could spend quality time together.

Livi was very pleased because things were moving along well. She had just talked to Ben who told her that he was seeing less of Marsha and Livi had already heard this from her friend Marsha who was upset at this change.

It now appeared that all of the work Livi was doing to get Ben back was working and she would be able to sleep well that night thinking it was now only a matter of time.

Hector went straight over to Livi's and was expecting her to be grateful. He found she was still awake and he related to her about what transpired. Livi did not say anything but she made an excuse saying she was tired, kissed him and asked him to leave.

Just as planned, the medication went into Beth's system slowly and took a while before it started to work. A noise in the hall awakened Beth and she did not feel right, starting to sweat and eventually starting to have trouble breathing. Beth looked for the nurse call button but could not reach it and was very fortunate that this happened just when Alex came to visit her. Alex entered the room and immediately recognized that Beth was in distress. She ran over to Beth, pressed the emergency button, and loudly shouted, "We need help! Call a code blue and bring a crash cart. "

It seemed forever but it was actually very quickly that the nurses came in and brought the crash cart. A number of staff came into the room as well as the doctor from the Emergency room but by then Beth had lost consciousness and stopped breathing. The doctor inserted a breathing tube, checked her heart rate which was very rapid, and her blood pressure was very low. The doctor called out that she was in shock. One nurse put EKG leads on her chest while another nurse did a finger stick to check her blood sugar. The level was only 20 which was much lower than the 100 where it should be. Beth was given a solution with sugar intravenously and in a few minutes her vital signs were improving. Fortunately they were able to save her life with fast diagnosis and treatment. Alex knew it was sheer luck that she had come in at that moment when it happened. Beth's other tests, including the EKG, X-rays, and a scan for a pulmonary embolus, blood clots in her lungs, were all negative. Alex realized how close she came to losing Beth.

CHAPTER 14

BETH TO ICU AFTER ATTEMPT

Beth was moved to the Intensive care unit and fortunately it was not long before she regained consciousness. Her oxygen levels were good and she was breathing on her own so the breathing tube was removed. Alex, the nurse and some doctors were there when Beth opened her eyes. Her vision was still fuzzy and she was somewhat confused but she was able to recognize Alex and asked her, "What happened?"

"Welcome back." Alex felt like crying but smiled, "Everything is good but you were out for a little while and we are trying to find out what happened." Alex realized how close she was to losing her best friend.

Alex stayed at Beth's bedside for a few minutes and waited until she was dozing off. Alex could not stop being grateful for having Beth back and thanking whatever divine intervention made her come into Beth's room when she did. Alex went to see the nurses on the floor by Beth's room and asked them "What happened? When did you last check Beth? "This was a question and not an accusation.

The nurse who was upset at what happened replied, "We checked her a half an hour before this happened when she was awake, laughing and seemed happy. Her husband was with her when I gave her the sleeping pill and he stayed with her until she fell asleep."

Alex questioned, "Did anyone else come in?"

"I don't think so. It was after visiting hours."

The emergency room doctor had asked about any medications Beth was given and he looked over her labs but all was in order except the low blood sugar. He could not explain how this had happened and questioned the nurse, "Why did her blood sugar drop so low? Has this ever happened to Beth before?"

"No and as far as we know and she was only given her sleeping pill."

The doctor reviewed Beth's chart and medication record and did not see anything to account for her low blood sugar. All of her lab results leading up to this incident were normal except from her blood loss when she was injured, for which she was given transfusions.

The staff started checking her blood sugar and her vitals every hour and then every two hours with the nurse in the intensive care unit watching her very closely. Her blood sugar was initially low but with the glucose infusion her blood sugar was stable. The doctor commented, "I don't understand it. Why would a healthy woman experience a precipitous drop in her blood sugar?" Pondering this, he went back to see his other patients.

Alex called Ben but did not reach him right away but she stayed close and available while she was finishing her rounds. She went back to be with Beth. She finally heard from Ben almost two hours later and he did not explain why he was unavailable. Alex did not say anything. Ben rushed to the hospital and waited in the visitor's room by the unit until he could see Beth.

The next morning Alex had to get back to work and had a meeting to go to but planned see Beth later. She could not understand what had happened and wondered if this had anything to do with the alleged car accident.

The hospital cleaning lady, Sylvia, came into Beth's to clean it since Beth was now in ICU. The room had been cleaned the day before including emptying the trash but it needed to be cleaned again for a new patient. Sylvia liked

'Miss Beth', as she called her because Beth was a very nice lady and always talked to her when she came into the room. Beth and she talked about their families and Beth always asked how she was doing. They talked and laughed about mundane things. She was very special to Sylvia because most of the other patients did not pay any attention to her except to make comments and give her instructions.

Sylvia was dismayed that Beth was not in her room this morning and she was concerned about her having to be transferred to the ICU. She checked with Beth's nurse and was happy that Beth was stable.

Just as Sylvia was about to change the trash bag in the wastebasket, she noticed a syringe partially covered with a piece of paper. She knew enough that this was not the proper disposal for a needle and syringe. Not putting a used needle into the red container on the wall placed her and other housekeepers at risk for being stuck with a needle and catching something. The nurses were carefully trained to prevent unwanted exposure by the careless disposal of a needle. Sylvia immediately went to report this to the nursing supervisor on the floor.

The nursing supervisor was suspicious because something had happened to Beth for which they did not have any explanation. The nursing supervisor asked Beth's nurse about the break in protocol for the disposal of a syringe and her nurse did not know about it. She said that Beth did not receive an injection or anything beside her sleeping pill since that morning. Given Beth's unexplained severe change in her condition, the nursing supervisor felt it was best to call the police. She always was worried about a nursing error harming a patient, which she believed was not the case so further investigation was warranted. She could not imagine anyone wanting to hurt Beth who was such a nice lady. She knew there was a protocol that had to be followed by the police when they collected evidence and hoped that an explanation could be found. She did hear that Beth was stable which made her feel better.

Fortunately Sylvia had not picked up the syringe and left it undisturbed in the wastebasket and had not cleaned anything else. The police came within the hour, put the evidence in a bag, and they tested for fingerprints on many of the surfaces in the room.

Beth was stable and feeling better so she was returned to a room on a regular hospital floor the next day. She was still recuperating from her severe injuries and was frequently checked to see if her severe relapse happened again. Alex came to see Beth and was pleased that she seemed to be in good spirits. Ok Alex thought, 'Good spirits' was an expression used to describe the mood of someone and chuckled at her questioning of a colloquial expression. But why did they say good spirits? And what did that mean? Was it comparing a good kind of alcohol to a bad one as though someone is happier after drinking a good alcohol and what did that have to do with Beth feeling cheerful? Alex chuckled to herself and dismissed her own questions thinking that the important thing was that Beth was doing better. Alex smiled at Beth and kissed her on the cheek as she was leaving. On her way to her car Alex started laughing when she thought, maybe I should stop off at a drinking establishment and have a 'good spirit' to celebrate Beth being on the road to recovery. And why did Alex now start to question the phrase 'road to recovery'? Stop it, Alex thought that this is enough because it is time for me to go home and get some sleep if I am able after what happened.

Chapter 15

Ben as a Suspect

When Beth woke up she realized that she was in the intensive care unit but fortunately she was told she stable and hoped to be moved out of the unit soon. It was difficult to sleep there as there was always activity, things beeping, and nurses checking her frequently. What she could see out of the small window in the room was that the sun was shining which made it a perfect day for her to be transferred to a regular hospital room, again.

Beth was happy as Ben was coming to see her every day because he was her life and she did not know what she would do without him.

Her lab tests were normal now although she was to remain in the hospital until her leg healed enough for her to get out of bed. Her leg was in a cast and still suspended due to the severe fracture and she was told that she had to be in the hospital a while. She spent her days seeing visitors and reading but the highlight of her days was seeing Ben.

Ben entered, kissed her on the cheek and said, "How do you feel today hon?"

"I am so ready to come home but they have me in this sling" and she smiled. "They said I am healing well and should be able to walk without a problem eventually, thank goodness".

Ben added, "That is very good news and I can't wait to have you home." He thought about Marsha who had been pressuring him to leave Beth but he was going to cease his contact with her.

Beth commented, trying not to seem too anxious, "I am happy you are back to the person I married because you changed so much before. We never discussed it."

Ben reassured her, "There is nothing to talk about so don't worry about it". He always avoided talking about anything that made him feel uncomfortable and especially about his feelings. He noticed the text he got on his phone from Marsha wanting to see him and he left the room to call her. He wanted to tell her now. "I am not going to see you anymore as I love my wife and she needs me now. You are a good person and I wish you well." Before he did not feel guilty hanging out with Marsha because he felt he was justified seeing Marsha after Livi convinced him it was best for him. He did feel guilty for not being available when Beth was injured and had her relapse.

Ben did not wait for Marsha's response as he went back to be with Beth who was his life now. He stayed with Beth until she started getting sleepy. He told her, "I am going home and I will see you tomorrow. Do you need anything?"

Beth replied, "I am good. Love you."

Ben said, "I love you too."

When Ben walked out and started down the hall there were two police detectives waiting for him. The taller younger one introduced himself and said, "I am Detective O'Connor of the county police department. Mr. Masters, would you accompany us to the police station? We have some questions we would like to ask you."

Ben was surprised. "I don't understand, concerning what?"

The Detective continued, "We cannot discuss it here but it does concern your wife Beth."

Ben was now concerned, "What about Beth" He did not get a chance to ask anything else as detective O'Connor pointed to the exit and said, "We had better go".

THE BOXES

The detectives were respectful and took Ben down the stairs to the back door where their car was waiting. Ben was too distracted to realize and appreciate that the detectives were escorting him away from the prying eyes and rumor mills of the hospital.

In the backseat of the patrol car Ben, was wondering why the detectives were going to question him about Beth and he was nervous about them escorting him probably to the police station. He didn't understand.

The police station was crowded with policemen, police personnel and others. There were a lot of people talking at the same time and it was hard for Ben to hear much until he was shown into an interrogation room. He was seated next to a metal table and there was a large glass mirror on one wall that he suspected was a one way glass for observation. He figured that there was probably at least one person watching on the other side of the glass while Detective O'Connor sat across from him.

He asked, "Do you know why we brought you in?"

Ben answered, "I am at a loss and I have no idea why I am here but I suppose you will tell me now."

The Detective responded, "You are here because you were the last person to see your wife in her hospital room before she collapsed and had to be resuscitated. Do you know anything about that?"

Ben was actually only a little surprised now and he responded "I know that she needed emergency care but I wasn't there when it happened.

Detective O'Connor added, "Yes you were called but it was several hours later that you responded. Where were you?"

Ben replied, "I don't have to answer that and why should that matter? I came to the hospital as soon as I found out."

He asked, "When your wife was hit by a car and brought to the hospital unconscious, the nurses said you were called did not respond until many hours later and the same thing happened with her collapse in the hospital as well. Why did it take you so long to respond to these calls?"

Ben answered again, "What difference does that make?"

Detective O'Connor went on, "Have you and your wife been having marital difficulties?"

"No one's marriage is perfect and there were some problems but we never talked about separating or a divorce.

We would have worked it out." However, Ben could not forget the terrible things that Livi had said many times to him about Beth and she had him convinced that he could never be with her. He also knew that Beth needed him now and he admitted to himself that he had been conflicted about Beth before but not anymore.

Detective O'Connor, watched for his reaction when he asked, "Who is Marsha Gregson?"

Ben thought he had been planning on leaving Beth anyway and had not been very discreet about careful about spending time with Marsha. Several of his their neighbors had actually met Marsha with him outside of his house and him now suspected that the detective had been talking to his neighbors. He felt that this was none of the detectives business and he was not going to elaborate about their connection. "She is only a friend."

When Detective O'Connor talked to friends and neighbors of Ben's they told what they had seen. They liked Beth and heard she was in the hospital and they were concerned about seeing another woman going in and out of the house. The detective said, "I talked to your neighbors about your association with a woman who is not your wife and they reported seeing her car at your house often. How long have you and she been friends?"

Ben now knew that the detective had done his homework. He now realized that the detectives were trying to establish a motive for him to harm his wife. He finally admitted, "Ok, so I wasn't immediately available when I was called about Beth's problems but she still gets very good care and I have seen her in the hospital every day."

The detective asked, "Does your wife know about your friend Marsha?"

Ben responded. "No she doesn't and I don't want her to know because it would hurt her. I already stopped seeing her."

The detective thought that if Ben was really worried about having a friend hurting Beth, then why he had one. He saw too many men that were selfish and self-absorbed like Ben and he added, "We know that your wife's relapse in her hospital room was not an accident and you were the last person to see her that night. Do you know anything about that?" And detective O'Connor had seen a number of situations where someone who cared about himself that much could justify harming someone who was in the way of what he wanted. And Beth was a very wealthy woman.

THE BOXES

Ben now understood why he was being questioned by this detective at the police station. They suspected him of harming Beth, especially since he was spending time with another woman. He asked, "Are you saying that you think I did something to Beth? There is no way I would harm her." He wanted to hear the detective's response.

Detective O'Connor looked at him and said, "I will be right back." He left the interrogation room and walked into the room where two other detectives were observing through the two way mirror. The detective asked the two observers, "What do you think? Do you think he is telling the truth?"

The older detective, said, "We have seen a number of married men with a girlfriend but that doesn't mean they try to get rid of the wife, but we have no way of knowing. However, we found about the financial problems in his businesses and Beth is a very wealthy woman whose assets are tied up in a trust, inaccessible to him if they divorced."

Detective O'Connor thought about this, and then asked, "Should we tell him about the syringe?"

The older detective said, "It is best that we not mention the syringe because he might ask for an attorney. Let's see what he volunteers first."

The detective returned to the room and told Ben, "You are not under arrest and we just wanted some information from you. Is there anyone that you can think of that would harm Beth and would you be willing to give us your fingerprints?" The detective was hoping Ben would do that and avoiding having to be booked to get his prints.

Ben was trying to help, "I have nothing to hide so sure."

Ben was taken to a fingerprint desk where there were a few unsavory appearing people getting fingerprinted as well. The process was quick and Ben was told he could leave the police station but he had to stay in the area.

A few days prior to Ben being questioned the police were given the syringe which was found in the wastebasket of Beth's room right after her collapse. They were looking for a match to the fingerprints on it and Ben was now their primary suspect for attempted murder. They just needed to see if the fingerprint matched his.

It took a few days to get the results from the syringe that was a clear thumbprint on it and the toxicologist found insulin in the syringe and needle. The police packaged it for evidence with the toxicology report of the content and an investigation showed that no patient that night was given any insulin. There were now police pathologists investigating what happened to Beth. Her symptoms could be explained by a possible injection of insulin into her IV which explained why any potentially fatal effects would not be noticed for a while. Fortunately Alex had come in just as Beth was reacting to the insulin.

It was not Beth's time to go.

THE BOXES

CHAPTER 16

CHANCE IN ALEX WAIT ROOM-CHANCE HX

Alex was in the office the day after meeting with Pete and seeing the photos of Ben with another woman which upset and she had difficulty concentrating. Fortunately she had an afternoon that wasn't too busy. She was a trooper and despite what was going on in her personal life she was always able to perform her duties well as a doctor. That was a skill she was good at and when she was very upset about anything, she went into her private office to cry but was able to put on a good front for the patients. She could walk into a patient's room, smiling and seeming happy despite how she felt. Her patients did need her and when her personal life was in shambles she had her practice to sustain her.

Chance was in Alex's waiting room thinking about his lunch two days before with his uncle Pete. He understood that he was here to help a lady doctor friend of Pete's. He thought and chuckled that coming into a medical office as a patient was a strange way to meet someone who needed his help. However, he would do anything for Pete since he was his best friend and his only family. He thought it was odd that he didn't remember Pete ever talking about Alex whom he said was such a good friend. That didn't surprise Chance as he knew Pete was always helping strays, people, animals and this lady doctor was another person that Pete helped.

While waiting to be seen by this doctor, his thoughts went back to when he and his uncle Pete had become close. Chance was the only survivor in the automobile accident that claimed his parents' lives. He was in his junior year of high school and just starting to look at colleges to attend. His whole life was shattered by his parent's death.

Chance's parents were both teachers and they lived in a modest but loving home with his mother involved in some ladies clubs and charities in her spare time while Chance's dad spent a lot of time with him. They went hunting and fishing and were able to spend a lot of quality time together which Chance appreciated. His first car was a modest older American car that they worked on together to get it running and look good. Chance was very proud of that car and he felt blessed, fortunate to have such a wonderful and close family.

THE BOXES

It was after church when the cement truck ran the red light that struck their car and Chance woke up in a hospital bed with no memory of what had happened. He didn't know how he got there but his whole body felt sore and he had a terrible headache. The light was very bright and he had bruises all over with his left almost swollen shut. He looked at the nurses who were quiet and said little. "Where am I and where are my parents?"

The older nurse who seemed to be in charge took his hand and said, "Dr Jones will be here shortly." She turned away so that he couldn't see the tears in her eyes. Although Chance felt a little fuzzy mentally, he became acutely aware that his parents were not with him and that no one was telling him anything. He was more aware now and asked again anxiously, "Where am I and where are my parents? What happened and why won't anyone talk to me?" He was very agitated.

Fortunately that was when Dr. Jones walked into the room accompanied by Chances' Uncle Pete, and when Chance saw the expressions on their faces, he knew why they were there. Pete sat on the edge of the bed and hugged Chance for a very long time and finally said, "You don't have to worry about anything because I am going to make all of the arrangements for what needs to be done. You are coming home with me."

Chance started crying and when he pulled back from Pete he looked at him, Pete was crying also. With the tears running down his cheeks, Pete managed a smile and said, "And for goodness sake, stop calling me 'uncle'. It makes me feel ancient."

That made Chance manage a weak smile which pleased Pete. Chance hugged Pete and through his tears he told Pete, "Thank you 'unc....., uh, Pete." He couldn't say anything else and was very grateful for Pete being there.

The little money left after his parents death was just enough to pay for their modest funerals. Being an only child and with his grandparents gone, the only family he had was Pete whom he had not seen much since both of their lives were so busy. Chance was busy with his parents and school while Pete was working or spending time with his wife.

Chance and Pete became very close and Chance knew how lucky he was to have him and his wife, Donna. There was a lot of laughter and love in their home and Chance became the son that they never had. Pete's wife even joked that the best adoption was a grown child that was already housebroken.

Pete was a good role model and he helped Chance get his bachelors degree plus his masters degree in criminal law at Rutgers. Pete and his wife also provided emotional support for Chance when he and his long term girlfriend, Helen, broke up.

Chance and Helen had been together through college and graduate school and Chance always though they would be married with a family. Unfortunately after completing her education in archeology, Helen had a different idea of what she wanted out of life. Her relentless pursuit of archeological quests around the world led them to grow apart and even though they loved each other they acknowledged that they had no future together.

Chance, Pete and Donna always made sure they were together for holidays. When Donna passed away it was like losing a mother again for Chance. Even when Chance was no longer living in Pete's house they talked all of the time and managed to see each other at least once a week.

Now in Alex's waiting room, Chance recalled why he was really here to see this doctor. Pete had called Chance and when he asked him to help with a case, Chance agreed right away, just as Pete did when Chance called him. When Pete started elaborating about this case, Chance's imagination immediately brought up images involving exotic places and people like the situations in the movies and although he knew that was unlikely, thinking about the possibilities amused him. Pete hadn't described the details of what he was working on because he didn't discuss things on the telephone, joking about 'hidden ears'.

Chance met Pete at their favorite Greek restaurant and they hugged each other. Chance smiled and said, "It's always wonderful to see you looking so prosperous and I see you have been enjoying life," indicating his uncle's protuberant belly and they chuckled.

Pete commented, "So I like to enjoy life." They both grinned." Pete asked like he always did when they saw each other, "How's the love life?" Pete always wanted his friends to be happy and as he had been so happily married, he was biased thinking a good marriage was the best situation to be in.

Chance answered, "I have female companions to go out to dinner and spend time with but no one I could settle down with. Wait he thought. Settle is not a good term because I don't want to settle. I am not impressed with the women I meet as they are either stupid or criminals. When people say they meet people at work, criminals are the women I meet." They laughed a long time at this. "Besides, if there was anyone special you know I would already have introduced her to you."

"That's what is worrying me because I don't want you to end up a crusty bachelor." This made them both laugh loudly again.

"Ok, let's talk about the favor you want. You said something about helping a friend so what is this about?"

"I do have an interesting case but there are things I can't find out. I discovered a lot but I am at a dead end so far and the lady involved is a special friend."

Chance raised his eyebrows and asked, "How special a friend?" And he smiled.

"She's not THAT kind of friend but we have known each other for years and helping each other out when the need arrives."

"All right. Tell me what you can." Chance was curious regarding how he could help this lady.

Pete related, "You know I can't discuss all of it because of professional ethics and I don't have all of the details so you should hear it from her. You are also looking good and it looks like you have been working out."

Chance answered, "You know I always do exercise and I think it would not hurt you. Now back to this case. What can I do to help?"

Pete started, "This lady, Alex, needs information and I told her I had a nephew who worked as a detective. I think you should meet her and the best way is for you to see her as a patient and ask her to lunch or dinner, so that she can tell you about what happened. Hopefully you can help both of us. She is a very nice person who is also single and cute."

Chance believed Pete only describing her as cute and nice, meant she was homely, overweight, or both. He knew his uncle often had ulterior motives and wanted him to meet someone and even introduced him to women but this would just be a favor.

"Alright. I will try to help and are you trying to fix me up?"

Pete grinned widely, "Would I do that? You are just going to try to help a nice lady,"

"Ok. I will make an appointment and what illness shall I have to go in?"

"A sinus infection works." Pete thought this was a diagnosis that could explain his visit.

Chance smiled at him and said, "Why not. I am open to new experiences."

He was now waiting to meet this lady to help her as a favor for Pete.

THE BOXES

CHAPTER 17

CHANCE- ALEX HISTORY-MEET ALEX

The day was sunny and warm and the flowers were in full bloom. Alex looked around her house with the sunlight streaming in and felt lucky to be here even though she had worked very hard to be in this life place. She had a very successful and lucrative practice although the money was not important because her patients were like her children that she genuinely cared about. Perhaps that is partially why she had such a busy and successful practice, but she was also very good at what she did. It was difficult for a female to be accepted into a surgical specialty, as there was still some prejudice against female docs so that is why she had to excel at what she did.

Alex also realized that being a good surgeon wasn't enough. Sean taught her that the hallmarks of a doctors success revolved around three things and she already had an idea what they were when he told her. They were availability, affability, and then ability. She often heard from patients who complained about previous doctors that although they were good, they weren't warm and friendly. They complained about being kept waiting to be seen a long time and the doctor did not explain things to them. Alex was available to see her patients when they needed her as well as being very skilled and knowledgeable. She also made sure she came to the office on time so that they were not kept waiting long. This last thing was important as it showed she respected her patients time by seeing them shortly after they came to her office. This especially pleased her patients. She received many referrals of friends and family from other patients which made her practice very busy.

Alex came from a modest upbringing and she worked very hard to get herself through college and medical school. She did get some financial help from her parents who had a comfortable but not lavish life. Her parents were not warm and close like she had observed in some of her friends' families. Alex's parents were more consumed with their social life with their so they spent little quality time with her. Her mother always advised her to find a rich husband but Alex wanted to achieve more than that for herself. She wanted to become a physician and help people. In the past her parents would be there if she ever needed anything but the long conversations and afternoons spent together with them were very rare. Alex did not feel like her parents understood her and her mother criticized her about numerous things. She could not confide in her mother without repercussions.

Despite this, Alex was still devastated by the car crash which took her parents lives while she was in medical school, which was just about the time she started seeing her fiancé. She had no siblings and was left a modest amount of money which paid the funeral expenses as well as her last year of medical school. Alex was always quiet and shy and gained some confidence in medical school, but that confidence was limited to her medical knowledge. She was not 'street smart', but she managed.

While Alex was in medical school she met Larry who was attractive, wise and seemed to provide what she lacked about life outside of medicine. The relationship was perfect until he turned out to be dishonest and an adulterer. When she met Sal he was also a strong person and helped her with things in her life she did not know how to handle.

After moving to Texas, Alex worked with another doctor for a year before she started her own practice. It did not take long before she was busy and able to pay off the loan she had taken out to start the practice.

Today was going to be a very busy day which was typical, and Alex always got to the office early unless there was an emergency. Within six months of starting her practice she was busy. That made her feel great.

Alex met Pete in her office, who started as a patient but became a good friend. She enjoyed their lunches or dinners together and he even tried to help her with her social life. He was a dear sweet man and she felt lucky to have him as a friend. Now he was going to help her and Beth with the accident.

Alex came into the office by the back door and went up to the front office to greet her receptionist as well as look at her schedule for the day.

Chance, Pete's nephew was in her office waiting room observing the decorations and furniture. He could tell a lot about a person by their surroundings and he liked what he saw. The waiting room had couches and comfortable chairs with lamps on the tables and indirect lighting instead of the awful fluorescent lights from the ceiling. The magazines on the coffee table were varied and current and not like the three year old worn copies he saw in some doctor's offices.

THE BOXES

The office was warm and friendly, like sitting in someone's living room and only a doctor that really cared about her patients would have such a pleasant waiting area along with a sweet and helpful receptionist. This was a good lady Chance thought, even though he had not met her yet.

Chance was to meet Alex with no idea what to expect except that he was seeing her to help her with a problem. He smiled thinking that because Pete told him she was cute so he did not expect her to be attractive. At least his uncle was trying to find someone for him to be with because Chance was now thirty four and Pete felt it was time for him to meet someone. Pete was always trying to fix him up which made Chance smile. Often when Chance was meeting Pete for lunch he was not surprised when there was a lady friend of Pete's who just happened to come by. Chance knew what Pete was trying to do even though Pete thought he was being very clever. He did not mind as he knew Pete just wanted him to be happy and he actually was ready for a serious relationship including marriage and children. Chance never stopped being grateful to Pete for taking him in as family when his parents were killed. He felt very lucky.

THE BOXES

The window into the office where the receptionist sat was open and Chance could see inside. A lady with dark hair came up to the receptionist to ask her something and when she looked up, their eyes met. He saw a beautiful woman with long dark hair and green eyes who was wearing a fitted green dress that revealed her very sexy figure. He was mesmerized and not able to take his eyes off of her. She went back to looking at the desk by the receptionist and Chance did take note that she was not wearing an engagement ring or a wedding band. She wore very little jewelry which he liked because he did not like flashy women. He wondered why women thought that jewelry enhanced their looks with the more jewelry the better. Chance could not look away from the stunning lady standing at the receptionist's desk until she walked into the back of the office.

Oh great he thought, because Pete was trying to introduce him to this lady doctor who needed his help and he was very attracted to one of her employees. He did not know how to handle this although he was going to try to help the doc for hers and Pete's sake. He was good at finding information and had a lot of resources to hopefully help her. Pete would not have asked for his help if this was an ordinary case and Chance was now curious about what was going on here. He did have an interesting profession with lots of different and unusual cases, but unfortunately there were lots of sad cases with things that no one should ever see. He had become hardened to a lot of what he was exposed to but every so often one of the cases affected him. He was human after all.

Chance filled out the forms and was taken into an exam room, while trying to remember what he had to say to be a legitimate patient. The medical assistant went over his medical history and he waited for the doc while he looked around at all of the equipment in the room.

Alex walked into the room and said, "Hello, I am Dr. Marsh and how are you doing today?"

Chance looked at her, stunned because she was the lady he saw while he was in the waiting room. She was now wearing glasses with her hair pulled back and a white coat that hid her figure. She looked very professional but what she wore somewhat masked her beauty. He chuckled to himself because this reminded him of the female superhero who hid her identity by dressing plainly with her hair pulled back and glasses.

THE BOXES

Chance lost his train of thought, forgetting what he was supposed to say and he had never been at a loss for words.

He blinked and swallowed and was able to muster, "Fine." He thought, fine? Fine was what everyone said when asked questions like, how is your family, how is your car running, how was your vacation or how did you do in the stock market?

Alex smiled and asked, 'If you are really fine then what are you doing here?" Now she laughed as did he. He was nervous and she knew that from experience that joking put patients at ease and she usually could get them to laugh which worked.

Chance hesitated before he spoke. "I have problems with congestion."

Alex, looked at his chart. "I see you said you are having problems with your sinuses."

"Yes I do once in a while." He knew he was exposed to some pretty bad odors from bodies at crime scenes which did not help. He looked up into her eyes which reminded him of deep sea green pools and didn't remember seeing eyes that color. He then caught himself thinking he had to pay attention.

Alex checked his nose and throat. 'Your sinuses look pretty clear and how often have you been having this problem?"

Chance started to feel a little more relaxed and answered, "Infrequently although my uncle Pete thought I should be checked."

Alex looked up from his chart at Chance. "Oh, you are Pete's nephew that he told me about and how is Pete? I assume you talked to him and he told me he was going to ask for your help. I guess we are helping each other and does helping you with your medical problem count?" She smiled and Chance noticed that she had a beautiful smile.

Chance smiled also. "Of course it counts." He was thinking that Pete did not adequately prepare him for Alex thinking that he thought it was funny only describing her as cute. She was light years ahead of cute.

Alex now realized that Chance had been put up to this with a flimsy medical problem as a way for him to meet her. She laughed to herself and thought, Pete you sly dog. Pete was a dear friend who thought she should fall in love and get married and he probably thought the same about Chance. This was not the first time he had tried to introduce Alex to men and the situations were not exactly blind dates but somehow nice men that Pete knew appeared when Alex and he were having lunch or dinner.

Alex was grateful to have a friend like Pete who just wanted her to be happy. Being close friends, she told him about everything in her past. He was just trying to help her be happy. She even told Pete somewhat about Sal and he was the only one she ever discussed him with besides Sean.

Alex was writing on Chance's chart and looked at Chance noticing that he was very attractive. She could describe him as dark and handsome, but he was sitting down so she could not tell if he was tall also. He had clear blue eyes with dark hair and even features who was the type of man to whom she was attracted. She surprised herself at what she was thinking as he was a patient and a relative of Pete's. She smiled to herself.

Alex dismissed her thoughts and began, "I know Pete said you could possibly help and I would like to talk to you about what happened, but I don't have much time to talk right now. I have a few more patients to see today which I won't be too long."

Chance suggested, "Would you like to have dinner someplace when you are finished? We can talk then unless you have other plans. Pete hasn't been able to tell me much. "

Alex said, "Sure. I don't have any plans and actually my schedule outside of work is pretty open." She chuckled and he smiled. She thought he was even more handsome when he smiled.

He was pleased when she said that and was still not able to get over how pretty she was. He remembered that Pete had mentioned that she didn't have any dates or a boyfriend. It pleased him to hear that although he had no idea what he was thinking. He thought, get over it because he was just here to help her.

Chance stood up and Alex looked up at him. He was very tall, at least six foot three and in good shape, muscular but not too much so. She again thought that he is very attractive and she liked tall men as she was fairly tall, five foot, eight inches. She couldn't believe that she even paid attention to that because it had been a long time since she even noticed anyone and now she had met two attractive men in a short period of time. She really wasn't dating Mike and she was only having dinner with Chance for help but what was she thinking?

THE BOXES

"I know this great Italian restaurant not far from here and does that sound good? I can meet you there. Does that sound good?"

"Who doesn't like Italian food and I will see you there, assuming casual dress is appropriate." She smiled.

Chance liked that she had a sense of humor and seemed easy going which was rare in so good looking a woman. He would definitely have to thank Pete because she was definitely more than cute.

Alex finished seeing her patients and went to the restaurant where Chance was waiting. She found Chance already sitting at a table at the back of the restaurant and Chance noticed the attention she as she walked towards him. The word that came to his mind about her was 'stunning'.

The restaurant was a charming old world style Italian bistro with red and white checkered tablecloths with flowers in empty bottles of Italian wines on each table. There were candles on the tables and the dimly lit room made for a very pleasant and romantic atmosphere.

"Nice choice" Alex said simply.

"I only go to the nicest places." And he laughed joined by her. They had a casual conversation about mundane but interesting things and the conversation flowed smoothly. The wine and the food were excellent and it wasn't until they finished the food that they started to talk seriously about why they were there.

Alex began. "I will give you the abbreviated version of what has happened. My best friend, Beth and I were run down by a car and I was hospitalized a few days for a concussion. Beth had severe injuries and while in the hospital, had a near-fatal collapse for which her husband is the primary suspect."

Chance said, "That is quite a history but I want to hear the details of what you just told me. I think you should know that I checked your history. "

Alex said, "You did? And what did you find out?"

Chance looked at her still mesmerized by her green eyes. He started, "I found out about your education history, that you have never been married, no children, where you lived before, that you don't owe anything on your house or car, are debt free, have never been arrested, have never even had a parking ticket, and you earn a nice living."

Alex was stunned and laughed nervously. "How do you know all of that? Did Pete tell you that? "

Chance answered, "Pete can't give me any of this information without your permission but the information I got is a matter of public record. You just have to know where to look."

Alex chuckled nervously and asked, "Do you do that with everyone? That must be tough on your dates." She laughed.

He chuckled. "No just on special cases because it's my job, ma'am." He laughed also. "I needed to know your background if I am going to be able to help you."

Alex didn't know what to say right away. She accepted that he knew all of the details of her life, but concerned that all of this information was available to anyone. Getting back to the reason why he was there, she related in detail about the night she and Beth had been injured, Beth's collapse, and what Pete had found about Beth's husband.

She was going to call Pete to tell him she was relating everything she knew to Chance and gave him permission to share all of her Information about this to him. However, she was going to request that he keep her personal past confidential.

Chance commented, "Beth is a very, very lucky girl that you came to see her when you did. Do you know anyone that would want to harm you or Beth or both? It doesn't sound like your altercation with the car was an accident, and I can find out what the police know which will tell us a lot more. I have a lot of friends on the force and access to everything they have by computer. We are waiting for the forensic results of the fingerprints found on the syringe used to inject Beth."

Alex was still worried about what happened. "Are Beth and I still in danger?"

"Don't worry as you are in good hands."

They finished their wine and Alex was surprised when she looked at her watch, "It's almost midnight and I have a busy day tomorrow."

Chance couldn't remember enjoying dinner so much although there were a lot of unanswered questions running through his mind. He was ready to call Pete and make fun of his 'cute' description. He walked her to her car. "Good night and thanks for joining me although the circumstances could be better. I will let you know as soon as I hear anything and would you like me to follow you home to make sure you get there safely? "

Alex looked into his eyes and could tell he was in earnest, a true gentleman and replied, "Thanks for the dinner but that is not necessary. I appreciate any help you can give me.

Chance watched her drive away thinking she was beautiful and did not realize it. He knew from what she told him that she really did need his help. He walked her to her car, opened the door for her, and said "Goodnight." He was looking forward to seeing her again.

THE BOXES

CHAPTER 18

ALEX BEAD-LIVI TALK TO BEN

The heavy rain and thunder was just starting when
Alex left the office and she had a patient to see in the
emergency room. There was a three year child there who
had stuck a bead into his nose and fortunately his mother
had not tried too hard to remove it. When a parent or
caregiver does that the child is traumatized before she even
sees him. That makes it substantially more difficult for her
to examine or treat if the child is hysterical. Alex thought of
the jokes about a husband trying to avoid having to call a
plumber to fix a plumbing problem and makes it worse by
trying which changes it from a minor problem to a large
expensive one. Alex realized that is the same with a bead in
a child's nose and a professional should be called first.
Unfortunately that doesn't always happen and if the child is
very upset and uncooperative then sedation may be
necessary, even to the extent of general anesthesia for
removal.

THE BOXES

Fortunately this was a better situation because the child's mother did not try to reach the bead lodged in her son's nose and took him straight to the emergency room. The staff at the reception desk was sharp and immediately had him brought back into an exam room.

Alex came to the hospital quickly and when she examined the child she saw that the offensive foreign body could be reached fairly easily. Alex mentioned to his mother that she was impressed that her son was so well behaved and was cooperative enough to allow a portable X-ray with her mother there. Alex had to make certain there was only one foreign body present and in this case there was only one. Back in the room in the emergency room, Alex explained to the mother, "The best way for me to remove it should not require any injections or anesthesia. We will put him on a papoose board for him to lie on with Velcro straps to immobilize him. Your son will complain about being restrained like this but I will be able to remove it very quickly." Just as Alex had said it only took a few seconds for her to secure the bead with a hemostat and remove it after which he was immediately released into his mothers arms.

His mother was grateful and relieved, "Thank you and I will put everything away so that he can't do this again." She was able to muster a weak laugh and Alex smiled.

Alex further warned her, "Sometimes a child that does this is more likely to do it again so keep an eye on him."

It was any easy quick fix for Alex which made her feel good but she wanted to see Beth as soon as possible. Beth had called her earlier and was very anxious, wanting to talk to her. Alex was concerned about Beth's call.

Beth was always relieved when she saw Alex who had a relaxed, comforting demeanor which made Beth and patients feel better. Alex walked into Beth's room and asked, "Hi. I see that your leg is still holding up the metal bar on the bed and how is the patient today?"

They both chuckled at Alex's corny joke seemed to relieve a little of Beth's tension but Alex could tell that Beth was very upset. Beth looked at Alex. "Ben was here and he told me he was escorted to the police station where they questioned him as he was the last person to see me the night you found me. He said the police did not actually accuse him of doing anything to me but they did fingerprint him.

Alex was silent for a minute and didn't relate what Pete had told her about Ben's female friend because she didn't want to upset Beth. She wondered if the police knew about her. There were so many questions in her mind but she was here with Beth to help her. Apparently they thought Ben had something to do with Beth's relapse but Alex knew he wouldn't have tried to harm her.

Alex said, "Don't worry and just concentrate on getting better because I am sure the police will find that Ben had nothing to do with any of this. Get some rest and you know that I am here if you need anything." Alex had to hide her concern and could tell that Beth was relieved. They hugged and Alex left.

Alex knew she had to call Chance since Ben had been picked up by the police.

Livi was home alone and was not enjoying herself because she felt that she should have been with Ben consoling him over the death of his wife. Now she couldn't think because all of her well made plans had failed.

Livi's phone rang and it was Ben. She was always happy to hear from him. He asked, "How are you doing?"

She responded as cheerfully as she could muster, "Find except for problems with the air conditioner but nothing new." In her mind she was screaming, no I am not fine because we were supposed to be together and you are clueless about how I really feel. She was not about to ask how Beth was doing because she did not want to hear how he was going back to her. She inquired, "And how are you?"

Ben responded, "Not so well."

Livi was never so happy to hear that, maybe... "I am sorry to hear that. What's going on?"

Ben continued, "I was taken to the police station for questioning and they even took my fingerprints. I don't know what's going on but they kept mentioning that I was the last one to see Beth before her collapse in the hospital. They know somehow about Marsha and although they did not say anything specific I can tell they suspect that I had something to do Beth's relapse. You know that I would never harm Beth."

Livi answered, "Of course you would never do that." Livi smiled and thought, you wouldn't but I would. She continued, "Is there anything I can do to help?"

Ben said, "I don't know but thanks for the moral support. They talked like they knew that what happened to

Beth was caused by someone or something and not a relapse. I don't know what to do."

Livi said "Don't worry although it might be a good idea to get an attorney." And she realized that the police not knowing who gave Beth something that could have been lethal, the circumstances pointed to him. It was just dumb luck that Alex came in just as Beth was reacting to the drug and saved her.

Livi thought, this is a turn of events because Ben could get convicted of attempted murder based on circumstantial evidence. He was the last one to see Beth, he did have a girlfriend, financial problems with his companies and if Beth died he would be a very rich man.

In her demented thinking, Livi was pleased that if Ben was convicted he could not be with Beth or anyone. That would be alright with Livi because if she could not be with Ben, then she did not want anyone else to be with him. It is not what she had hoped for but she could live with that. She would still be his friend and maybe when he got out he would turn to her. She was patient.

Ben was nervous. "Are you still here?" Livi had been lost in thought.

THE BOXES

Livi responded "I am here for you no matter what happens and you know that. You know that if you need anything at all I will help." And she thought, except help you with evidence that can exonerate you.

THE BOXES

CHAPTER 19

ALEX AND CHANCE, CAR, BEN SUSPECT

It was a long day for Alex with her morning of surgeries starting at 7:30 followed by seeing her patients in the hospital. She had just enough time to eat a sandwich for lunch on her way to the office to see patients. She enjoyed her work as she was helping people and it was very rewarding but very time consuming. Being busy and it also kept her from thinking about the past. She was grateful for her mentor, Sean taking a chance on her and accepting her into the residency which made her the first female surgery resident. She smiled that she was an innovator, a groundbreaker and in a wonderful life place.

Alex was glad she was busy because it kept her mind off of her concern about what Chance was going to tell her since he had mentioned that he had found out some information about Beth's relapse.

Alex didn't want to admit it to herself but she was looking forward to seeing Chance which was crazy she thought. Here Mike, who was attractive wanted a relationship and yet she was looking forward to having dinner with someone who was a purely professional contact. He was going to pick her up at her house which she thought showed her he was a gentleman.

Chance was very impressed with Alex from the first time he met her in her office because she was beautiful as well as very accomplished. Her attention and care she showed for her patients was obvious and he respected her for that. When they had dinner and talked about business, he found her to be very down to earth with a sense of humor.

Under different circumstances he would have considered asking her out but he knew it wasn't appropriate. Tonight he had a lot of things to tell her which found out through his work. He found himself really looking forward to seeing her again. He almost felt like an excited teenager which made him chuckle at himself.

He went to her house and she greeted him at the front door. She said, "You are on time but come on in, I need a few more minutes to get ready." Chance walked into Alex's house and looked around, seeing that it was very warm and comfortable like what he felt in the waiting room of her office. This was a home and he could see her touches everywhere. The rooms were large with high ceilings and a lot of windows. He liked what he saw and he could see that it was a safe haven for her from the world. He knew he could tell a lot about someone by their home and this place suited her.

He sat down on her couch which he noted was very comfortable and not like some that were for show. Yes he thought that this was a real home.

Alex quickly finished getting ready and came out, "You look comfortable. Would you like a drink?"

Chance replied, "Another time but thanks. I will just have something at the restaurant." He hoped that maybe he would be invited there another time and then corrected himself asking himself about what was he thinking. He reminded himself that this was professional and he smiled at his thoughts.

He looked at Alex when she came into the room and felt like whistling. Alex wore a fitted. Burgundy silk dress with her dark hair gleaming even in the subdued light and she was radiant when she smiled.

"Where are we going?" She looked at Chance.

THE BOXES

She never thought to ask before but she wore a nice dress that worked no matter where they went. Chance was wearing a nice suit and he looked very handsome.

Chance replied, "You will see." He would enjoy being seen with her in addition to being with her and it had been a long time since he had felt that.

They arrived at the Fish Market which was a place that was not large but intimate and very cozy with very good food. Alex was pleased at his choice and noticed he had even reserved a booth in the back. He was so attractive she thought, but she had to concentrate on why they were there. Chance ordered a good bottle of wine, made a recommendation when they ordered, and they exchanged pleasantries while they ate. After that he became serious and started relating what he had found.

"I discovered a great deal but I will start with the car that hit you and Beth. I don't think you were told that the police got blood and samples of the clothing that you and Beth were wearing when you were hit by the car. It was just lucky that the police impound employees do an occasional check of the cars in the lot and they found a car there that had no record of being placed there. They do know it was not there three months ago when they last inventoried the lot. Research on the car showed it had been sold several months ago at an auction and there was no record of who bought it except that it was purchased for cash."

Alex paused and then said, "I don't understand. What does that have to do with Beth and myself?

"There was a small amount of blood and hair wedged in the bumper of the car that had not washed away from the rain and the hair and blood matched Beth's. It was an older American car with no fingerprints which meant that the inside of the car had been wiped clean. However they did find a matchbook under the seat." He waited to see her reaction before he went on. She was pale and silent. He continued. "The matchbook was from a club where a lot of nefarious characters and mafia bigwigs hang out."

Alex was trying to understand what he was saying. "Alright. What does that mean?"

Chance replied. "It makes me feel that there is a possibility that whoever was driving the car may have been there and possibly hired to hurt or kill you or Beth or both. This makes me think that this was no accident, especially since the car was carefully cleaned and put in a place where it would not be noticed for a long time. When it was found it could not be traced."

Now curious, she asked, "Then how did the car end up in a police lot and what about the security on the lot. What about cameras?"

Chance nodded his head, "Yes they have cameras but the tapes are on a continuous loop recorder and record for only two weeks and the recording starts over. That means that after two weeks whatever was on the tape is gone. So basically there is no record of when or who put the car there but we believe that it was the car that struck you."

Alex let that information sink in before continuing. "With the tight security on the lot, how could it get past the security and what about the employees that were watching the lot?"

Chance related, "We thought of that but unfortunately, when we tried to find the employee or employees working around the time you and Beth were hit, there was a confusion in the scheduling and no one remembers anything. I don't know but I suspect that it involved someone that had connections or influence with the police. There is definitely some corruption around a lot of places and the people that hang out at that bar where the matchbook is from have a wide reaching influence. It happens and all it takes is money. "

Alex looked into his eyes, "I guess I am ignorant of what goes on except what I see in movies," and she laughed a nervous laugh, "But it sounds like someone went to a lot of trouble and why harm me or Beth. Is it possible that Ben hired someone and isn't he a suspect for Beth's collapse at the hospital?"

Chance continued, "We already ruled out Ben as a suspect for the incident in the hospital. A syringe cover and a syringe were found in the wastebasket by Beth's bed and the syringe had a small amount of insulin in it. The fingerprints on the syringe were not Ben's. They belonged to a petty criminal who a thief was named Hector Gonzales. He was off probation and allegedly working as a handyman and we are working on finding him. Does that name ring a bell?"

Alex responded, "Yes insulin could have caused what happened to Beth. I don't know Hector. But the name does sound familiar. Wait! Beth may have given me his name when I needed a handyman for some work around the house and I don't know if Beth ever hired him. When she gave me the phone number a while ago she said Livi told her he was good. Of course that was when Livi was still talking to Beth. I am not certain what happened there and I don't think Beth understood it either. I think I have his number on my phone." She found it and gave it to Chance who could tell she was upset even though she tried to hide it. This was a person who could not play poker as she was too transparent with what she was thinking.

Chance said, "Thanks. Getting his phone number will help a lot."

Alex now inquired, "Then does that mean that Ben is no longer a suspect?"

Chance answered, "We have not ruled him out completely although we did check his bank records and there were no unaccounted withdrawals so he did not pay anyone to harm Beth. And I hope you don't mind that I am still communicating with Pete and he said Ben was no longer seeing Marsha."

Alex did not know what to say. She was happy that Ben was no longer a suspect and he was spending a lot of time with his wife. She was glad his extramarital friend was gone. Her elation rapidly changed to dread when the realization struck her. That meant that someone else was trying to do real harm to her or Beth or both. She became frightened and she looked into Chance's blue eyes and asked him, "Since we are now pretty sure that someone was trying to hurt us and we don't know who or why, are we still in danger?"

Chance looked into her clear, green, mesmerizing eyes and replied, "We thought about that and although we now know Hector's name, we still are not sure if anyone else was working him or hired him to harm both or either of you. We do have a police guard at the hospital with Beth and I wanted to talk to you about your safety."

Alex paused before she could respond because the threat of real danger was frightening. She looked at him and tried to understand this, "Do you think I am in danger?"

"I don't want to frighten you but that could be a possibility."

Alex tried to hide her fear and finally said, "I admit that I am concerned but I don't want a police bodyguard and my house is secure with an alarm."

Chance offered, "I was hoping you were going to invite me over tonight to hang out for safety and I could spend the night on your couch." That idea pleased him especially since women like chivalrous men.

"Thank you for your offer and I will take it under advisement." Alex smiled when the thought occurred to her that she would not mind having Chance around for protection although her mind immediately countered, 'stop that'

It was late when they finished their meal and the bottle of wine. Alex usually did not drink much, but with the news she heard, she helped Chance finish it. She was still shaken when Chance took her to her house and insisted on looking around to make sure everything was secure.

Chance knew staying at her house was for protection and not romance although he would have liked more time together on a personal basis. He had given a lot of information to Alex and he could tell she was concerned and a little frightened but he did not want to stress it which could scare her more. She said, "Thanks for helping and for your concern."

He walked her to her door and said, "Goodnight and call me if you need anything or even to talk." Alex shook his hand and he went to his car where he stayed a while to see if there was anyone around the house.

Alex was more concerned than she was willing to believe about any danger but still could not think of why anyone would want to harm her or Beth. There was no one she could think of that she or Beth had any fights with or even any disagreements. Finally, she thought, this is enough for tonight.

Alex was exhausted both physically and emotionally and she tried not to think about anything. She would wait and see what Chance discovered. She already hadn't been sleeping well and this would interfere with her rest more. Thinking about sleep aids, she thought a large carbohydrate load like a large bowl of ice cream before bed could help. She started thinking about home security like a gun or maybe a very large dog but not now. She chuckled at where her mind was wandering which did help to relieve some tension and she was finally able to fall asleep.

CHAPTER 20

HECTOR TO POLICE STATION

The next day, Chance went to the police station and checked his desk to see if there was anything urgent that he had to address. He kept thinking of Alex and what an enjoyable evening they had even though he had to go over some uncomfortable news. It was better for Alex to know what he had found out at least and his concern for her safety. He wanted to help protect her which of course meant spending more time together. He laughed at himself and thought that would be very difficult but he could probably force himself to do that. With Hector's fingerprints on the syringe used on Beth in the hospital, it was time to bring him in for questioning.

After Beth ended up in the ICU, Livi told Hector that they could not see as much of each other to avoid suspicion and that they had to hide their relationship for a while but only for a brief time. He believed her when she told him that now that Beth was no longer trying to evict her and he thought he could move into her place. Now they could be together forever and even get married. This made Hector happier than he could ever remember.

The police didn't find Hector at his apartment but they did have his cell phone number. Chance sat down at his desk in the police station to call Hector and arranged for a recording of the conversation while one of his colleagues listened in as well. He was hoping Hector would answer and hopefully he had tracking on his phone so that they could tell where he was.

Hector answered his cell phone right away as he was between jobs, "Hello, who is this?" He didn't recognize the phone number but he was used to getting calls for work, and he definitely needed some employment.

Livi called out from the other room, "Who is that honey? I need your help moving this picture."

Hector responded to Livi, "Just a minute sweetheart."

Chance asked, "Is this Hector Gonzales?"

"Yes this is me."

Chance started, "I need some things done at the house and I got your number from a friend of Livi's." Chance didn't lie because he did need some work done around his house although he said 'the' house when he talked to

Hector, so it could mean any house. The call was being recorded so he had to make sure what he said was fairly accurate in his conversation. He thought that most criminals were easy to catch with properly prepared strategy like this situation.

Hector was happy to get the call for a possible job. "I could help you but what part of town are you in? I only work in the city or the suburbs that are close."

Chance and the other officers had to quickly scramble to find a house close enough to Hector for him to be willing to come which only took a few minutes. Hector hoped it would be a big job so he could get something nice for Livi. Chance gave Him his first name and the information about the location of the house and Hector agreed. They arranged for a time to meet. Chance easily obtained an arrest warrant for Hector based on the evidence they had and he would not be happy to find some uniformed officers waiting for him at the house.

When Hector left Livi's home he was happy at his good fortune to get a job to earn some money and help her. He smiled and thought that life is good and especially since he and Livi were going to be together.

THE BOXES

Since Beth's relapse Livi had substantially decreased the amount of time she and Hector spent together because she had only tolerated Hector to get rid of Beth. She was now actually ready to eliminate him completely from her life now that he served his purpose but unfortunately he failed. Livi could not risk another attempt at Beth so she even started paying Hector for work around her house including getting receipts so that it did not look like they had a personal relationship. She still allowed him to stay at her house but rarely.

The next morning the wind was blowing and the shutters were rattling at Livi's house. Hector woke up next to Livi and looked around, admiring the high ceilings and beautiful paintings on the walls. He could hear the chiming of the crystals hanging from the chandelier and on the balcony. It was an old house and smelled a little musty from time but he was happiest here. Many of the furnishings in her place were carved dark mahogany and cut glass crystal handed down to Livi from her family. He felt at home and he was always happy when he woke up next to her. He felt she needed him and he would do anything to make her happy.

THE BOXES

Hector felt very good when he thought he was helping Livi by getting rid of Beth which would solve her problems but unfortunately Beth survived. He thought it was odd that Livi was not more upset about Beth's survival of her collapse in the hospital. Livi explained that Beth being in the hospital for a while made her back off about having her evicted and although it would not have made sense to anyone else, Hector blindly believed her. He knew Livi was grateful to him for trying to help her but he could not understand why she had suddenly become too busy to see much of him even though she still said she loved him. He accepted it and felt they would soon go back to like it was before.

Livi was still asleep while Hector quietly dressed so that he would not disturb her. He left to go to the job he had been called to do and was happy to earn some money to help her.

It did not take him long to find the address he had written down and he was pleased that it was in a neighborhood with large well-kept homes. The streets were clean, the lawns were well manicured, and there were expensive cars in the driveways. He walked up to the front door of the house and rang the bell thinking this could be a good job for him. He looked around and there was no car in the driveway and he wondered if anyone was home. He heard a noise behind him and was surprised to see three policeman standing there. One told him, "Put your hands in the air and don't move. We have a warrant for your arrest."

He complied and one of them handcuffed him and read him his rights as he was ushered to a patrol car. Hector was very upset especially since he had been convicted for stealing and breaking and entering in the past but he had been lucky with little prison time. However even though he did not know why this was happening, it seemed more ominous.

Hector, handcuffed, said to the policeman from the back seat of the car, "I don't understand. What is this for?"

The policeman said, "You are under suspicion for assault and attempted murder."

Hector was not thinking clearly and tried to understand what was happening. He replied, "I did not do anything." He could not say anything else.

It seemed like a long ride to the station house even though it was close. Hector was booked, fingerprinted, and shown into one of the sterile rooms they took people for questioning. Detective Schultz sat at the metal table across

from him and asked Hector, "Do you know Beth Masters?"
Hector suddenly realized what his arrest was about and he
did not understand how they knew about what he did. No
one noticed him in the hallway of the hospital or saw him
go into her room. He had made sure Beth was asleep so no
one saw him inject anything into her IV. He left her room
and the hospital without anyone around which went
perfectly the way Livi had planned it. Nothing went wrong
but he was here and wondering how they knew it was him.

Hector was questioned and answered that he did not
know anything. He was told he could make a phone call so
he called Livi, "I am at the police station. I was arrested
and I need your help. What should I do?"

Livi answered, "What happened and why were you
arrested?" Livi wasn't sure but she did not want to take a
chance that the conversation was being recorded. She
continued, "I don't understand why you are calling me."

Hector was rattled because he never expected this. This
was very serious and he was afraid to give details to Livi.
"They asked me if I know Beth Masters but I did not say
anything." He asked again, "What should I do?"

Livi was much shaken and knew she had to protect
herself. Her mind was racing and she needed to handle this.

Even though she believed that Hector would protect her there was still a doubt in her mind. Worried about the police listening to their conversation, she said, "I am not a friend of Beth and I don't know what is going on. Whatever is happening with you it good idea to ask for an attorney. They have to provide one for you free and don't say anything until you talk to the attorney." She said this coldly and was careful since she was certain that there wasn't anything concrete to prove she was involved. After all, he was the one who actually suggested that he go to the extreme measures to get rid of Beth and she made him believe that it was his idea.

Livi had believed that Ben was still a suspect for Beth's collapse in the hospital. Whatever the police knew, she had to make certain that there was nothing to connect her to Hector or Beth's breakdown. She also knew that Hector was not very clever and she was concerned that he was the weak link, the way the police could get to her. Livi was very experienced at manipulating people and she had worked on Hector so that he would protect her at all costs even though the police were experienced at getting information from people. She already had him convinced that his attack on Beth was to save her from what Beth was allegedly doing to her and now she had to keep him from revealing anything.

With Hector at the police station she realized that Ben was probably no longer a suspect which meant that he was going to be with Beth. All of the work she did by hanging out with Hector and guiding him to help her did not work. She looked around her place which was her home, but she was alone again. She had been looking forward to being the one love in Ben's life but she was never going to give up and the important thing now was that Ben did not find out that she had a part in harming Beth.

Hector requested an attorney and he was placed in a holding cell while one was contacted. The station was crowded and people were moving around which gave him time to think. Whatever happened he did not want to go back to jail and it was important that he protect Livi in all of this. He knew the sentence was worse for a repeat offended but who would take care of Livi if he was not around?

Hector had been in a cell like this before and fortunately his attorney, Fred Ward was able to see him that afternoon. When his attorney came in, he knew little of the circumstances why Hector was arrested but wanted to talk to his client. Hector of course denied any knowledge of why he was arrested. His attorney had done this often before and could tell that Hector was not telling him the truth.

Fred introduced himself. "I am your attorney if you like and as I see it, I am the only one that can help you. You have to tell me what happened and I mean everything, because this is the only way I can help you. I know that there is some concrete evidence implicating you so I want you to tell me the truth."

Hector still denied any involvement "I did not do anything and the police don't know what they are talking about." He was shocked that they had evidence against him.

Learning nothing, Fred told Hector that he would have to wait in the holding cell while he got a report of what the police had found. At the desk of the detective researching the case he identified himself as the attorney of record for Hector. After a short wait he received a copy of the report of the specific evidence against Hector as well as the printouts of Hector's arrests, convictions, and his time in jail. The report had what the police lab found in the syringe as well as Hector's fingerprints. He gave a low whistle and returned to his client.

Hector was shown into the small room where an attorney could talk to his client in privacy.

Hector was nervous and asked, "What did you find out?" He was hoping that they were mistaken about the evidence.

Fred looked at Hector. "You have a real problem." And he proceeded to show Hector the evidence the police had against him. "Now I think it is time for you to tell me the truth about everything. What you tell me is attorney client privilege which means that I can't tell anything to anyone without your permission. Can we talk?"

Hector was blindsided and had trouble believing what he heard but there it was on the papers Fred showed him. He realized he was in real trouble. He had to talk to his attorney but he still wanted to protect Livi and wondered how he could do that. How could he help her if he was in jail and yet he could not dispel his fear of going back?

Several police detectives took Hector into another room and started tag teaming Hector with questions, some of which were repeated but worded differently. His problem was threefold. First, his fingerprints were on the syringe with the insulin and whether they could prove that he actually injected it mattered little because it showed some involvement or complicity in what happened. Secondly, the injection was not an accident. There were no orders for the medication and it hadn't been administered by any of the medical staff. Based on Beth's reaction to the injection it was a potentially lethal dose. It was only chance that Alex came in right at the critical moment to save Beth.

Thirdly, there was no ascertainable motive on Hector's part including no record of money exchanged for him to do this. The only connection that they knew of was Livi who gave Beth and Alex his name for some odd jobs.

The detectives repeatedly questioned him for hours, trying to get him to tell them something.

Detective Schultz asked, "Where were you the night of October 4th?"

Hector replied, "I am not sure but maybe at my local bar having a drink."

The detective continued, "Did anyone see you there who can account for your whereabouts that evening".

Hector answered, "I don't know." He was starting to get upset and tired. His previous answer was at a bar and now he was saying he did not know.

Detective Schultz felt he was getting closer to what Hector knew. He asked, "Do you know Beth Masters?"

THE BOXES

Before Hector could answer, detective Schultz continued, "Have you ever been to Memorial Hospital?"

Hector was now very nervous because of the repeated questions about Beth and he was starting the think they knew more than his connection to the syringe. He replied, "I don't know her and I was not at that hospital, that night or ever."

Detective Schultz was experienced at questioning suspects and could tell that Hector was nervous about Beth and the hospital. He knew the only connection although distant was to Livi and him now suspected that there was more to this. The police obtained a record of Hector's phone calls after they arrested him and found many phone calls to and from Livi. Fred asked Hector "What is your relationship to Livi and how do you know her?" Detective Schultz observed Hector's panicked reaction to these questions and realized he had hit the jackpot.

"Livi is a friend and I did some work for her." Detective Schultz could tell there was a lot unsaid based on the many phone calls and the evidence. Hector would not say more so the detective had Hector go to the cell where he was being held. He sent out some detectives with a photo of Hector to Livi's place to talk to her and the neighbors to learn more of their involvement here.

Livi's neighbors were quick to volunteer information because it seemed that Livi was not well liked. They said she was moody, unfriendly, frequently complained, and three of the neighbors confirmed the frequency of Hector's visits to Livi. They said Livi seemed close to Hector as she kissed him goodbye when he left. This information was reported to detective Schultz who now had someplace to look about what happened to Beth.

CHAPTER 21

QUESTIONING LIVI HER HOUSE

Detective Schultz knew that Hector called Livi after he was arrested. She was obviously a close friend and he felt he could get some information from her so he went over to her place to question her about Hector. He knocked on the door and when she answered he identified himself. He asked, "Can I ask you some questions about Hector Gonzales?"

Livi had to keep her panic under control when she found out who he was because she knew Hector was at the police station and this was not good. She did not know what to do and thought the less information she gave, the better. She tried to appear calm when she said, "He did some odd jobs for me but really don't know him well and we have nothing to talk about."

Detective Schultz was still outside her door and said to Livi, "We can talk here or we can do it at the station house. It is your choice."

Livi couldn't think of any way to avoid this and finally agreed, "You can come in."

He entered noticing some elegant furnishings and oak wood floors. The decorations were of fine glass that had once been valuable and a beautiful antique rug that had seen better days. Her place was fairly large and comfortable. She looked old and was wearing poorly matched clothing that did not fit her. Her makeup was excessive and she wore a lot of costume jewelry. He didn't think she was attractive at all.

Livi indicated he could sit down but did not offer him anything to drink, thinking his questions would take very little time.

Detective Schultz got right to the point, "Do you know Beth Masters?" When Hector had called she did not think that he had said anything about her but this line of questioning was very disconcerting to her.

Livi replied, "Beth was a friend although we had a falling out a while ago."

"How well do you know Hector and have you been spending time with him.....socially?"

Livi could tell he knew something. "Well we have been spending some time together but he is just a friend." That sounded like a good answer to her.

Detective Schultz could tell she was not telling the full story and he needed to know more such as how close they were and how Beth fit into all of this, if at all.

Detective Schultz watched her reaction when he told her, "Several of your neighbors mentioned that Hector was at your place often which included some morning departures, and you were affectionate in public. Are you more than just casual friends?"

Livi had to think about how to address this and she finally responded, "We were just friends and I don't know anything about Beth. Are we done?" She thought she had handled this well.

Livi thought about the conversation she had with Hector when he called from the police station and it was pretty generic. She had been too careful for the police to get any proof of her involvement so she now thought that even having an affair with Hector did not matter. The only connection between Hector and Beth of course, besides him trying to kill her, was the referral from Livi to Beth for work around the house. Even if Hector said something about her it would be her word against his. After all, would they believe a convicted felon over an upstanding citizen like herself and if he told them what she said about Beth, it was all untrue. Beth did not own the building she was living in and Livi had plenty of money. This was easy.

Livi admitted, "Yes we did have a close relationship but what I do with my personal time is no one's business. I have nothing more to say."

Chance knew that Livi was being questioned by the police about Hector and he knew what the police knew. However he wondered what the motive was for Hector to give the insulin to Beth and the police could not prove anything.

Chance was having dinner with Alex that evening to see if she thought of anything else that could explain what happened to Beth. He thought about Alex who was a happy, attractive person and he wondered why she did not have a boyfriend. He was certain that a lot of men would like to be with a beautiful, intelligent, and financially sound lady. He questioned why there was an attempt on hers and Beth's lives, and so far they hadn't found anything in either of their pasts that would explain it. He finished the paperwork at the station and went home to change.

THE BOXES

CHAPTER 22

HECTOR IN POLICE STATION-ADMISSION

The police station seemed more hectic and crowded than usual. Hector was in the holding cell and frightened. He did not want to go back to jail and he knew he was being charged with some serious offenses which could mean a long sentence. Hector was waiting for his attorney and was happy when Fred came back to see him. Now he realized Fred was his only chance of freedom and he would have to tell him everything.

Hector was taken to a private room where Fred could talk to him.

Fred asked, "How are you doing and can we talk about what happened? The police have some incontrovertible evidence against you and you are looking at a lot of years for assault and attempted murder even if you were only an accomplice. I hope you understand how serious this is."

Hector already knew how serious this was. He told his attorney everything including his relationship with Livi and how he offered to help her.

Hector finally said, "I really love Livi and I only wanted to help her. Livi had told me how Beth, the lady in the hospital, had stolen her husband and gotten all of their money including the building that Livi was living in. Livi told me that Beth was going to evict her and she did not have any money to go anywhere else. She was very upset and was crying all the time about it."

Fred thought about what he said and asked, "How did you get from wanting to help Livi to attacking someone in a hospital bed?"

"Livi explained that as long as Beth was around she was going to lose everything including her home. I knew that Beth had to be stopped and I don't make hardly any money so I could not help her."

"So you wanted to stop Beth but whose idea was it to go to the hospital and inject Beth with something to harm her? I assume that is what happened."

"I wanted to help her and Livi actually told me what to do."

Fred was hearing what he suspected. "What did Livi tell you to do?"

Hector explained, "She told me to dress in dark clothes like my shirt with a hood and wait until no one was outside the hallway of Beth's room. She said the best time to go was in the evening when there weren't a lot of people there. I was supposed to get a bottle and a syringe off of the cart the nurses push around and then go into Beth's room to inject the stuff into the bag hanging by her bed. Livi had a bottle and a syringe at home and she taught me how to get the water into the syringe. After that I was supposed to wait until the hallway was clear again and leave. She said that the stuff would take a while to get into Beth so I had time to leave before it worked. I didn't understand that but I just did what she told me to do."

Fred was astonished. "Are you telling me that you did this to help Livi and she planned everything like how you were going to do it? Did she actually want Beth to die?"

Hector shrugged his shoulders. "She never told me to kill her but I knew this was bad. Livi was crying and said this was her way to be safe from Beth."

Fred asked, "What did you do when you injected the drug?"

"It was easy 'because Beth was asleep. This was to save Livi. She said what Beth did was ok with the law and there was no way to help her. I put the stuff in the bag and then I heard noise in the hall. I was afraid to be caught with the plunger so I dumped it in the wastebasket. I didn't think anyone would see it because it was trash. I waited and when it was quiet outside, I walked out slowly like I was supposed to. The only person I saw was a lady with long dark hair who got off the elevator when I was about to go down the stairs and she didn't see me.

Fred said, "Then Livi actually planned what you did to Beth and is there any proof she did that? Did she write it down anywhere?"

Hector answered, "No she said she didn't want to write anything down and kept going over what I had to do so that I could remember it."

Fred realized that Hector was not clever enough to plan what happened to Beth and his motive was based on lies Livi told him. Fred was in communication with the detectives researching the case before he saw Hector and they showed him that Livi not only owned her place but had plenty of money. Fred didn't know what Livi's motive was to harm Beth but she found a person to do it for her with nothing to connect her to the crime. Fred thought she was very clever to let Hector be blamed and his only chance was for him to connect Livi to what happened.

"Hector, do you realize that what you told me about Livi planning what you did makes her an accomplice and if we find proof or if she admits to what she did, your jail time can be reduced. She convinced you to inject Beth by telling you things that aren't true. The police investigated her and they found out she owns her home and has a substantial amount of money."

Hector was silent. He did not understand at first but he slowly realized that he harmed someone that may have been innocent. He was confused because he loved Livi and believed everything she told him. He finally said, "I don't understand why she said that and are you saying she lied to me?"

Fred was trying to be as gentle as he could, "I am afraid she did. Can you think of anything that would link Livi to what you did such as phone messages or anything written down? "Fred was fairly certain that Livi would carefully hide her involvement, even letting Hector be blamed and prosecuted for this.

Hector continued. "She kept going over everything I was supposed to do many times because I had trouble remembering things." He paused, trying to remember and finally said, "Livi wrote down some things I needed to know on a piece of paper. Let me think. She wrote down the address of the hospital and Beth's last name so I could find her and there was something else. Oh yeah, she also wrote down the name of the stuff in the bottle that I was supposed to get because I couldn't remember it."

Fred inwardly smiled because this was something concrete. He asked, "Do you remember what you did with that paper?" He was hoping that Hector still had it.

Hector thought about it a while and finally said, "I think it is in the pocket of the shirt I wore when I went to the hospital. I forgot that Livi told me to throw it out."

Fred tried to be calm when he asked, "Where is the jacket?"

"I put it on the chair when I got home because I was going to go to Livi's. When I called her she said to not come over. I don't remember why. I used to see her most days but now she says she is very busy. I don't see her much."

Fred said, "The police can get a warrant to search your place and do I have your permission to tell the police about the piece of paper? It might help you."

Hector would do anything to try to stay out of jail. He replied," "Sure. The shirt is black."

Fred said, "I am afraid that you have to go back to your cell but I will meet with you again soon."

Fred immediately called the police detective who was investigating this case and he told him what to look for at Hector's place. "This could be some important evidence and I am certain that you will make sure any fingerprints are undisturbed."

The detective thanked Fred for the information and when he asked Fred a number of questions He replied, "I cannot talk about it now but there may be another person involved."

Detective Schultz said. "No problem and we are leaving shortly to look for the jacket."

Fred hoped that the police would find evidence that could help Hector who was a simple person who fell in love with the wrong person and had been used for her own agenda. Now he had to find out what her motive was for the sake of his client.

THE BOXES

CHAPTER 23

BETH QUESTIONS

It was time for Fred to talk to Beth and perhaps she could tell him something that would help his client. Even though Fred was appointed to be Hector's attorney, he worked very hard to help him like he tried to do with all of his clients. Fred felt badly for Hector as he now thought that Hector had been convinced to harm Beth by someone who took advantage of him.

He needed more information about Livi and thought Beth might have information that could explain Livi's motive to harm Beth. Hector had been trying to protect Livi and although he knew what he did was wrong, he believed that it was to help her. He didn't understand why she lied. Hector was a simple person and had a previous conviction for burglary but he was not a murderer. Fred knew Hector had no medical training and it made sense that Livi had instructed him regarding the medication and the injection. Livi had been very careful to avoid anyone having any real evidence that would involve her, but Fred may have found something. Fred called Beth at the hospital who agreed to see him.

Fred went to Beth's room and found her to be a lovely blonde lady with a slight build. She was lying in her hospital bed with one leg in traction for her injuries and Ben was with her sitting at her bedside holding her hand. Beth was awake and although Fred could tell she was in pain she did not complain. Fred read people well and he could tell she was a good person.

Fred said, "Thank you for seeing me and as I said when I called you, I am Hector Gonzalez's attorney. He is the man who gave you the injection that almost killed you. Do you know him or can you think of any reason he would try to harm you?"

Beth paused, surprised, and replied, "I remember his name from Livi who recommended him as a handyman but I never hired him. That was before Livi stopped talking to me and I can't imagine why he would do anything like this to someone he doesn't know."

Ben said, "I don't know him either and did you find any reason why he would do such a thing?" He nervously looked at Beth to see if this was upsetting to her but she seemed fine.

Fred went on, "I can't really say but Beth, why she stopped talking to you?"

Beth tried to force a smile and said" I don't really know because she had been a good friend of Ben's and we became friends after Ben had introduced us."

Ben added, " Livi and I were closer before I met Beth but we are still good friends. She told me a lot of terrible things about Beth when we started seeing each other and even said we were not right for each other."

"Livi said the same thing to me about Ben. She criticized his lack of formal education and his history of dating, calling him a womanizer. I never told Ben or paid any attention to what she said because I loved Ben from the beginning." She now realized what Livi was doing.

Ben looked at Beth. "I never mentioned what Livi said and she even told me that you did some terrible things to her. That was when she stopped talking to you and I am now ashamed to say that I started believing her. That changed the way I felt about you for a time. I can't believe that I trusted her and could not understand why a friend that I had known so many years would say something unless it was true. I thought she was trying to protect me and I regret that I listened to her. I now know that she told you and me awful things about each other because she did not think we should be together. She also said terrible things about the other ladies I dated in the past.

Fred listened closely, "Can you think of a reason why she would do that?"

Ben said, "I never wanted to hurt Beth with what Livi said and I now know it was false. However with what happened I can guess the reason. When we first met years ago she clearly indicated that we were perfect for each other and she wanted to be my girlfriend but I was not interested. I was never more than a friend to her. I guess she thought that she and I should be together."

Beth said, "I never heard about all of this but Livi did pay a lot of attention to Ben. I always thought she was just a good friend to him and myself. I remember her complaining that Ben did not talk to her as frequently when we became a couple and that she rarely saw him. Perhaps she thought I was interfering with her relationship with him. I realize now that she was never a true friend to me. Alex said that a real friend does not stop talking to you no matter what happens. She said friends may have disagreements but they get over it and stay friends."

Ben nodded in agreement, thinking about the reasons Livi had told him that she was no longer a friend to Beth. It did not make sense to him at the time but he did not want to get involved because Livi was still his friend.

Fred now thought that this was Livi's motive to get rid of Beth. If Beth passed away, Fred wondered that Livi was thinking that she would be there for him to comfort him and would have him to herself. Livi planned to get rid of Beth and got Hector to carry it out. She tried to make sure there was nothing to connect her to what Hector did and he was pretty sure that she did not care if Hector took the blame and went to jail. He also realized that when Ben was a suspect she did not come forward to help. Was it possible that Livi did not care if Ben was in jail to get him away from Beth? He dismissed that thought because without proof this was only conjecture.

Ben was holding Beth's hand and Fred could tell that they obviously loved each other.

Ben asked Fred, "Is there anything else you need from us?" He was still holding Beth's hand.

Fred answered, "No but thanks for your time and here is my business card if you can think of anything else. Feel free to contact me any time."

They said goodbye and Fred left. Now he had to wait and see if the police found the paper in Hector's pocket at his place.

THE BOXES

CHAPTER 24

LIVI EVIDENCE-ADMISSION

Fred had to be in his office the next day and he couldn't stop thinking about his client, Hector. He felt sorry for him as he was probably a pawn and was going to take the fall for something he had been convinced to do. There was no question that he was guilty but fortunately Beth had survived. Fred had seen so many unfortunate things involving his clients as a court appointed attorney but this one bothered him. It was a shame.

The next morning the sun was shining with sparse clouds and the temperature was warm. This was a beautiful day to be outside. Fred thought it would be an even better day if the police lab turned up something on the note from Hector's jacket pocket.

The police detectives had a warrant and went to search Hector's apartment which was shabby with very little furniture. They found the piece of paper in Hector's pocket with Beth's last name, the supplies he was supposed to get and the address of the hospital. Wearing gloves they

250

carefully placed it into an evidence bag to take it to forensics.

Fred was due to see his client Hector and he hoped to have the results on the paper by then.

Fred was happy when he received a call from the detective investigating Hector's case, "This is detective Schultz and I thought you wanted to know that we found Hector's fingerprints on the note we found in his pocket but there is another set of prints on it as well. As it turns out the handwriting on this paper does not match Hector's." Fred was very pleased because this was good for his client.

Detective Schultz went on, "But we don't have Livi's fingerprints or a sample of her writing. With Hector's phone bills we can establish at least a friendship with Livi who is apparently now a suspect and we are going to bring her in for questioning."

When Detective Schultz called Livi and asked her to come to the station, she answered, "I don't understand why because I told you Hector and I were just friends. There is nothing I have to say about his activities."

Detective Schultz now explained, "I am afraid if you don't come voluntarily, we will have to get a warrant to bring you in."

Livi was anxious, although she was certain they had nothing to connect her to Hector about what happened to Beth. She was very careful to avoid any evidence about the attack but she wondered how they could get a warrant for her unless Hector said something. Trying to become calm she called Ben and asked him to take her to the station. She said it would be fast as it was just routine and she needed some support. Ben agreed since he was always around to help her.

Detective Schulz saw Livi when she came in and asked for him. She was overweight with dark shoulder length hair, medium height, and dressed in cheap looking clothing that did not fit well. The dress had a low neckline that showed the tops of her breasts and was too tight around her large stomach making her look even larger. Fred thought the heavy makeup she was wearing, her high heels, and the way she was dressed made her look trashy. Livi had not aged well and she looked much older than her actual age. The detective introduced himself, "Hello, I am detective Schultz and I am in charge of the investigation of what happened to Beth. Thank you for coming in." And he turned to Ben and said, "And you are?"

THE BOXES

Ben looked at him and responded, "I am Ben, and a friend of Livi's and Beth is my wife. We have no secrets from each other. Livi asked me to come along and why is it necessary for her to come in?" Fred realized that this failed attempt for Livi to look sexy was for Ben.

Livi told Ben her version of what happened and although he was sympathetic, he wondered why the police wanted to talk to her. He knew her long enough that he could tell there was more to this story than she was telling him. He wondered if this involved what happened to Beth.

Detective Schultz said to Livi, "Please come with me." And he took Livi to one of the interrogation rooms knowing this interview was going to take some time.

Livi sat down at a table across from detective Schultz who came in with two cans of soda. He opened both and handed her a can while being careful to avoid touching the sides of the can he gave her.

Detective Schultz said, "I thought you could use some refreshment while we discuss a few things." She drank from her can and put it down in front of her after which he carefully picked up her and replaced it with the second can. He told her, "Make yourself comfortable and I will be right back."

THE BOXES

Livi did not know what was happening but did not think anything of his odd behavior. A lot of thoughts ran through her mind and although she hoped Hector would not say anything about her, he may have. She had not talked to him. She was not worried however, as she was sure they would not believe him over her. After all it was the word of a convicted felon against hers. She was certain this session would not take long.

Detective Schultz returned and sat down again. He was calm and did not show any emotion and he said to her, "Do you know why you are here?"

Livi smiled, and replied, "I have no idea." She was starting to get a little nervous but she knew she could not show it.

The detective began, "First of all you have not been arrested for any crime but we are going to record this interview. We just want to talk to you about Hector and what your relationship was with him. Do you have any knowledge how he knew Beth?"

Livi saw the mirror on the wall in the room and suspected that there was someone watching this interview and she replied, "We are just friends. I gave his number to

Beth for some work around her house and I don't know if she called him."

Detective Schultz felt he had to step up the interview and see if Livi would confess to what happened. He said, "We found Hector's fingerprints on the syringe with the medication that was administered to Beth that almost killed her."

Livi wondered how they found that but still tried not to show any emotion. She was now upset with Hector for being so stupid to allowing the police to find something with his fingerprints on it. Obviously the police suspected that she was somehow involved or she would not be here. Hector must have talked about what happened and she started inwardly panicking. She paused to think of something to tell the detective and said, "Hector never told me what happened except that he was arrested. Also I heard from a friend about Beth's accident but I didn't know about any relapse. I don't know anything else."

Carl questioned her, "Can you think of any reason why Hector would want to harm Beth?"

Livi tried to remain calm and answered, "I have no idea." She was pleased that she had been careful to avoid any evidence of her involvement.

THE BOXES

Carl was ready to confront Livi with what the police had discovered. "What if I told you that Hector said he harmed Beth to help you because Beth was going to evict you and had harmed you financially? And what if I told you that Hector told us that you planned the attack on Beth and he directed us to a piece of paper on which you had written Beth's last name with the address of the hospital. The police found the paper with two sets of fingerprints on it. One set was his and the other was from an unknown person."

Livi responded, "That is ridiculous as my finances are good, and I don't know anything about any paper." She was starting to panic. She was now very angry at Hector because she told him to destroy that paper and if he had, she would not be here.

Carl continued, "We are working on the source of the second set of fingerprints and I think I should tell you our forensics lab now has the can of soda that has your fingerprints on it. They are processing it now. That proof can show a connection to you for this crime. If you were involved and want to confess what happened it can go easier on you, or you can take your chances in front of a jury."

THE BOXES

Livi lost her composure when she knew she was trapped. They had proof of what happened and she could not lie her way out of this. A jury would look at Hector who was a simple person that tried to kill Beth because of her lies and the proof that she planned it. She tried to think of anything that could help her now but there was nothing. Her only chance of leniency was to confess and make a deal.

This was over and Livi said simply, "I would like to make a deal."

"That depends on what you tell us."

Livi confessed. "Yes I was involved." And she realized that now Ben would know what happened but being her close friend, she was certain that Ben would understand why she did it and forgive her. He would not turn his back on her.

Carl knew that Hector would still go to jail as he did the attack but his sentence would be reduced because he was unduly influenced.

Livi was quiet and in shock. Carl finally said, "Is the reason you wanted to harm Beth have anything to do with Ben?" He was already pretty sure based on what he had heard about the conversation with Beth and Ben.

Livi now was angry and upset. All of her work including her meticulous planning and putting up with Hector to get him to do the attack was for nothing. And now she was in trouble and was worried that this could change her relationship with Ben. Ben was hers and neither Beth nor anyone else could have him and she blurted out, "I was doing what was best for Ben because I am the only one good enough for him to be with. We have been friends for a long time and he wouldn't listen to me when I told him Beth was wrong for him. And then he had to marry Beth! This was the only thing I could do to save him! I am his best friend and he knows that."

This confirmed that Livi's obsession was the reason Beth was harmed. He thought it was unfortunate that although Livi planned everything, Hector would still be convicted for the attempt on Beth's life. At least now he would not have as severe a sentence.

Carl went into the waiting room where Ben was sitting patiently talking to Beth on his cell phone. He hung up when Carl walked in. Ben asked, "Where is Livi?"

Carl replied, "I am afraid that Livi has been arrested for her involvement in the attack and attempted murder of your wife. She confessed to having planned it and getting her friend Hector to carry it out."

Ben sat for a while to process what he had heard. At first he could not believe it but realizing it was true made him think about everything that had happened.

Ben knew he had initially been the primary suspect in the attack on Beth until they got evidence exonerating him. For a very uncomfortable time he did think that there was the possibility of him being convicted just on circumstances and especially since he was the last one to see Beth before she relapsed. The police knew that there was a very large amount of money for him to inherit if something happened to her. It would have been so easy for Livi to mention her involvement in what happened to Beth to save him. He now realized that Livi would let him be convicted for something he did not do to protect herself.

Ben had known for a long time that Livi wanted to be close to him but he thought she was happy being just friends. He was only mildly surprised about what Livi did because he knew that she was capable of doing what she needed to get what she wanted. However, he would never have believed that she would resort to murder to be with him. Ben was very hurt by what transpired and upset with himself and Livi because during his lengthy friendship with her, he never realized how evil she was. She was never his friend.

When Livi was taken into custody and led past the waiting area in handcuffs, she looked for Ben but he was not there. She was silent realizing her friendship with him was over.

CHAPTER 25

MIKE DINNER

Alex was awakened early by the loud thunder and she didn't know if she could go back to sleep. In the past waking up next to Sal had made her feel safe and nothing bothered her including terrible storms. But that felt like a long time ago even though it had been only a few years before. She looked outside and it was not raining hard but there was a lot of loud thunder and lightning which made her uneasy although she could not explain why. This made her chuckle thinking this was ridiculous as she was an adult, not afraid of snakes, bugs, or rodents which frightened most people, but she had a problem with storms and especially the ones with thunder and lightning. It was curious for her that when she was involved with Sal she always did feel safe even when he was not physically with her.

Now she was on her own again and when she had lost her trust in men, Sal restored it. He treated her as a priority and with respect which she really appreciated. He never lied to her and he made her feel good about herself. She jumped out of bed to get ready for a wonderful and busy day.

Mike called her or texted her at least once a day and Alex liked hearing from him especially since he seemed like a good man.

Alex met Mike at a local Chinese restaurant and they had a pleasant conversation, with just talking about mundane things. It was helpful that Mike was also very handy and when Alex needed a lightbulb changed or a closet door fixed, he was always willing to help. She liked having him around as a friend.

They went for dinner a few times and Alex was just happy to get out because she was starting to feel like a recluse. She even invited him over for dinner twice which she did infrequently as her home was a place of solace and safety for her. She rarely invited anyone over even to pick her up or drop her off.

The first time Mike was at her house she had given him a tour and he was very complementary of the house and the way she decorated it. One of the things he commented on were the unopened boxes he saw in one of the spare bedrooms. She smiled and changed the subject. The second time when she had invited him over for dinner he again mentioned that the boxes, "I noticed that you still haven't opened the boxes in your back bedroom. What is in them?"

Alex did not think anything of this, and replied, "They have some mementos from the past and I still haven't gotten around to sorting out the contents. There is no hurry."

Mike remarked, "Well your place is definitely large enough to have room for a lot of things and you shouldn't have to keep things in boxes. I have time and I can help you if you want."

Alex replied, "I appreciate the offer but I am alright with the boxes being there." Alex thought that his offer was just an excuse for Mike to come over to her house again although she felt a little uncomfortable about the attention he paid to the boxes. She thought watching a movie might take Mike's attention away from the boxes.

Mike responded, "I understand. I stopped by to see Beth, and her spirits are good especially as her husband was there. They seem very happy."

Alex wasn't sure what to think but she hoped he was right about them being happy again.

Thinking of Beth reminded her that she was supposed to see Chance who called to report that he had some more information for her. She wanted to hear what he had discovered.

Mike was sitting in the chair next to Alex and he decided that it was a good time to talk to her about the time they were spending together. Alex noticed that he now seemed to have difficulty conversing with her as though he was trying to get the courage to talk to her about something important. He finally said," You and I are friends, but only friends and we enjoy each other's company. Do you feel anything more than friendship?"

Alex thought she would be surprised but she had a feeling this was coming and she replied, "I hadn't thought about it and I do value our friendship but I am not interested in anything more." She knew she was attracted to him but hadn't been open to having a close relationship with anyone. Although it had been some time since she had been with Sal, he was still fresh in her memory.

Mike knew that Alex hadn't been dating as they talked a lot about what they were doing all of the time and he commented, "I have talked about my past relationships and my ex-wife but you never talked about yours. Perhaps if we talked about your past I could help you work through things. Also, I noticed that you seem very touchy about the boxes you have been avoiding in one of your bedrooms and does your aversion to being more than friends have something to do with the contents of the boxes? I know you are very organized and it surprises me that you haven't emptied them. I am not saying that I am a womanizer but women seem to want to date me. They seem to find me attractive and you know I am a nice guy with a good sense of humor. We obviously enjoy being with each other and I really like you but I want to know if we can talk about the possibility that there is a problem here interfering with us progressing to a different level.

Alex laughed nervously, "I never thought I had a problem but I just need to get to know someone before I get involved." Alex knew she had a problem but she was not about to admit it and this was starting to get too complicated. And there was something she could not ascertain about Mike that made her feel uncomfortable so she was reticent about getting involved with him. She couldn't explain what it was about him that bothered her but there was something. He was almost too perfect being tall, very handsome, healthy, educated, no children, caring, and with seemingly little baggage. It was as though he had been dropped out of the sky. He never talked about his background or family except that he had been divorced, sometime and he had no friends here although he said he had been working in the area for a while. Mike did not seem to date and was always available to her.

Mike smiled and said, "I thought that is what we have been doing and getting to know each other but is there someone else?"

Alex said, "I haven't been seeing anyone else socially which you know, and my best friend is in the hospital. I have a busy practice and I work a lot of hours." Now she was starting to feel uncomfortable with all of his questions and although she did trust Mike in a limited capacity she was still afraid of really trusting someone again." I enjoy our friendship and I like you but I still need some time."

Mike commented, "No problem and I will give us some time to see where this goes. It was a great dinner so let me help you clean up and we can call it a night."

THE BOXES

While Alex was finishing putting the dishes into the dishwasher Mike picked up the dish towels and asked, "Where can I put these?"

Alex was cleaning the counter and had her back to him, "Put them on top of the washing machine in the laundry room and I am impressed by your domestic side." She smiled. "You would make someone a very good wife." This made them both laugh.

They kissed each other on the cheek when he left and Alex was wondering why he kept mentioning her unopened boxes. Did he think she was hiding something? The repeated attention to these boxes was very curious and she thought about putting them in a closet out of sight. There was nothing valuable in these boxes. She kept a diary while she was with Sal because she wanted to remember every precious moment when they were together although a lot were etched into her memory. It was a happy time for her with no pressure and never any criticism like she had experienced from her parents and her ex fiancé.

Alex took a lot of photos on the boat when she as with Sal including everyone and everything to better to remember their time together. Sal had a lot of friends with their extramarital girlfriends as well as people he did business with but she did not pay attention to any of that. The women were pretty much bimbos and more interested in what they received from their patrons, like money, furs and jewels. Alex did not care about the material things. Sal gave her a lot of the same types of gifts and she wore some of them when she was around his group to please Sal. Sal appreciated that she was a very classy lady which he remarked to her often.

The contents of the boxes included things like napkins, place cards, and matches were from restaurants they had gone to. The boxes that were still at Beth's were the ones with her diary and the photos from when she was seeing Sal. She wondered if she might be too sensitive and paranoid about Mike's seeming interest in the boxes.

Alex dismissed all of this as she had a lot of other things to think about like nearly being killed by a car, Beth's collapse, and a question about Beth's relationship with her husband.

When they finished cleaning up, Mike gave her a kiss on the cheek and left.

CHAPTER 26

BREAK IN

Alex awakened at eight in the morning which was late for her and the day was already a cheerful, sunny day. She could smell the coffee that was ready thanks to the timer she had on the coffee pot. She walked outside and stood on her patio with her coffee while admiring the flowers and the clear sky. There was a gentle breeze and she could smell the scent of the flowers and see the branches of the trees swaying from the wind. She had a busy day scheduled but she was distracted by what Chance was going to tell her and also by the nice evening she had spent with him.

Then she thought about Mike who was a good man and wanted a relationship with her but unfortunately she did not feel the same. He always offered to help her with anything she needed but there was still something about Mike that made her feel uncomfortable. She couldn't identify what it was, however.

The phone rang and it was Mike who asked, "Good morning and how do you feel today?"

She responded, "Good especially since I slept well and I am ready for my busy day."

Mike called for more than a greeting, "How did your meeting with Chance go and what did he find out?"

Alex described very little of what Chance had told her, and asked, "How have you been?"

Mike responded "Good, but nothing exciting. Did Chance say anything else?"

"Not much other than what I told you. Enjoy your day." Alex didn't know why she didn't want to tell him more and she went back to seeing patients. Alex's day was very busy as expected but rewarding since she liked helping people. It started raining heavily on the way home which was not a major thunderstorm although driving with the excess water on the roads was a challenge. She looked forward to going home, letting her hair hang loose, putting on some pajamas and just hanging out.

It was after dark when Alex walked into her house and she had an odd feeling that something was not right. She did not notice anything out of place right away when she walked in but she had an uncomfortable feeling. Her bedroom was downstairs and she rarely went upstairs but she started looking around. She was about to climb the stairs when she noticed that there was a light on. She came from a poor background and her father had always told her to make sure she turned out all the lights which she was careful to do. She never left any lights on upstairs.

Alex was frightened and worried that someone had been in her house or may even may still be there. She hurriedly grabbed her keys and her purse and ran out to her car. She sped away and drove to the parking lot of a nearby busy restaurant while checking to see if she was followed.

Alex called Chance. "I need your help because I think someone broke into in my house and may still be there."

Chance told her. "Calm down. Are you alright?"

"I am alright but shaken up. I only leave one light on downstairs but when I got home, an upstairs light was on." She now thought that Chance was right about having some security.

Chance commented, "Where are you and are you in a safe place? I am coming to get you and I am calling some patrolmen to come to your house. "

Chance found Alex at the diner and she got into his car. "Do you want me to take you someplace or do you want to come with me to your house while the patrolmen are checking on it? You could wait in the car while the police go in."

Alex replied, "As long as there are police there we should go to my house for me to see if something is missing or wrong." Alex was silent as they drove there. She was frightened and did not know what to think.

There were two police cars with four policemen at her house when she and Chance arrived. Chance greeted them and they reported that they had already gone around the house and didn't see anyone suspicious outside or in the neighborhood. They told him the doors to the house were locked and they said they did not see any cars there or any movement inside. Alex agreed to check the house with the police. She was nervous when she walked up to the house with Chance and several of the officers, unlocked the door and stepped aside for the others to enter. The police went in cautiously with their firearms drawn while she waited outside and a few minutes later they came out to report no one was inside so it was safe for Alex to enter.

Chance turned to her to see how she was doing, noticing that she was very pale and anxious. He asked, "Are you alright? You do know you don't have to go into the house." But he knew from experience that if she did not go in right away she may be afraid to go in at all.

Alex took a deep breath and said, "I'm ok to go in." she was trying to appear brave but Chance knew differently. Alex went in slowly and checked the downstairs reporting, "My jewelry is intact and there doesn't seem to be anything of value missing. I like looks like someone opened the cupboards in the kitchen and some of the books are out of place on the shelves of my office. However the window in the laundry room is open and I always keep it securely latched."

Chance looked at her again to make sure she was alright although she looked rattled. He was proud of her for how she was handling the situation but he knew she would break down afterwards. He asked," Are you sure you are able to look around more?"

Alex replied with a forced smile, "Sure because after all, I have five strong armed men with me." And she laughed nervously.

She followed Chance upstairs and they looked in all of the rooms noticing that the light was on in the room where she had kept her unopened boxes. Chance drew his gun and went in first followed by several policemen who also had their guns drawn. They also checked the rest of the rooms. The tape sealing the boxes had been removed and the contents strewn around. The two closets were open as well. Chance asked Alex. "Were these boxes closed?"

"Yes they were and sealed with tape."

"Can you tell if there is anything missing?"

Alex looked around at the contents of the boxes on the floor, "I am not sure although there really wasn't anything valuable in the boxes except papers and mementos. No one would care about those." As soon as she said that, it occurred to her that Mike had asked about the boxes a number of times.

Chance told Alex, "Whoever was here may have gotten in through the open window in the laundry room and the alarm which was also in the laundry room was disabled. We checked the locks on the doors and they seem intact. We are going to fingerprint the whole house and check for footprints outside that window. You said the window was always locked so is it possible that anyone could have opened the window? Has anyone been in that room?"

Alex replied, "My housekeeper but she has a key. She would not do this." Alex thought and realized, "Wait a friend of mine who is a paramedic was here for dinner and took some dirty dish towels into the laundry room when he was helping me clean up."

Chance inquired, "Who is this person and how long have you known him?"

"Mike is just a friend and he is one of the paramedics who came in the ambulance the night Beth and I were injured. That was the first time we met. I was fuzzy from my injuries and I ended up in the waiting room for the emergency department. He found me there and took me to the back to be seen as a patient where I was treated for some lacerations followed by being admitted for a concussion. He did visit Beth and I a few times in the hospital and he gave me a ride home from the hospital when I was discharged. He seemed like a nice man and often called to check on me. We did go out to eat a few times as friends and he has been here twice for dinner. I thought he was a friend but it was curious that he asked me about the boxes a few times and repeatedly offered to help me open them."

Chance continued, "Didn't that strike you as odd because who cares about a few ratty cardboard boxes?"

Alex mentioned, "It seemed odd to me but he seemed alright and always offered to help me with whatever I need around the house."

Chance asked, "Do you know anything about him, like where he came from or how long he has been a paramedic?"

"We never talked much about our past other than him talking about a former girlfriend."

Chance asked further, "So what is your relationship with him?" Chance had to be careful with how he asked this. He barely knew Alex but somehow he couldn't believe he was jealous about her seeing someone.

Alex answered, "As I said, we were just friends and we talked once in a while. He did say to me that he wanted to be more than just friends but I told him I wasn't interested in anything more. In fact he called wanting to see me today but I declined because I had a very long and busy day scheduled. "She watched Chance's reaction and thought she could tell what he was thinking which was probably what she was thinking. Did Mike have anything to do with what happened today? However she tried not to believe that and dismissed it. Chance noticed that Alex was nervous and stressed and the impact of this break in still hadn't affected her.

Alex finally said, "I need to get some rest as it is almost midnight and this has been a very stressful day. Fortunately I don't have any surgeries scheduled tomorrow and I am going to cancel my afternoon patients because I need a day off, or maybe six months. I can't think but I know I am afraid to stay here tonight. I don't know what to do." She looked at Chance for guidance.

Chance took her hand to make her feel better and said "I understand because what you are feeling is a common reaction. However you may not feel secure at a hotel unless there is a policeman there but I think you will feel alright here with several policemen for security. You will be safe here and even if you go somewhere else you will still have to face coming back here sometime. What do you want to do?"

The thought of having to pack a bag to go to a hotel seemed like a lot more than she wanted to do or even think about. Alex sighed, "As long as there are policemen here I would prefer to stay in my own home." Alex did feel violated. There had been a stranger or strangers in her house and she wondered why only the boxes seemed to have been tampered with.

The police left and Chance stayed until a female police officer got there. Alex talked to Chance about mundane things and was grateful that he was there. She felt very safe with him and appreciated the way he took control of the situation. He was very wise and was right knowing that if she left her home she might be afraid to come back. When Grace, the police officer got there Chance left but on the way out he asked Alex, "Can you think of anyone that would be interested in what you had in the boxes to go to this much trouble?"

Alex replied, "I can't think of anyone right now but my thinking is fuzzy. I will be thinking more clearly after I get some sleep and hopefully I can. Goodnight and thank you for your help. I am impressed and grateful at how you handled this situation."

Chance looked into her eyes and replied, "No problem and tomorrow we will check your house for cameras or bugs that should not be here. We can pick up your car in the morning." As he was walking to his car he thought about Alex who beautiful inside and out. He really liked this lady and was looking forward to spending more time with her.

THE BOXES

He was very worried about her safety because there was more going on here than the obvious, and he wondered who this Mike person was. The next day he was going to do an extensive background check on him.

Alex called Cassie to explain what happened and to cancel her patients. Alex was mentally and physically exhausted after all that had happened but she still looked around her bedroom, bathroom, closets, and even under her bed to make certain no one was there. She did feel violated at the thought of someone being in her house and going through her things. Finally, in her bed she was going to try to fall asleep. She thought about Chance and she understood why having a man in the house made it more secure which would make her feel safe. Her mind kept going over things that had transpired such as the injury, and did the thief find what he or she was looking for. She was trying to relieve her tension and joked with herself, 'It is a good thing I got rid of the government secrets'. This was so absurd, that it made her laugh out loud which was exactly what she needed right now. She was trying to relax enough to fall asleep which happened faster than she expected.

CHAPTER 27

MIKE AND GINO

Mike was not looking forward to this meeting with Gino. He failed to find what he was told to get and he was now worried for his life.

Mike recalled his life several months before he was at the accident where he met Alex. He was in another city, happy, and things were going well. Unfortunately his life was about to change and not for the better.

Mike was what some people might call a gigolo who had been very successful in getting money from women he met while working in a hospital when they were there visiting family or friends. These women were very upset at the time and they appreciated him being sympathetic and helpful. He was skilled at rapidly determining which women were wealthy and easy marks. Being tall, fit and attractive was a good asset for this skill he had, and he easily convinced them that he was a nice trustworthy person who would help them in a time they really needed emotional support. He got many times more money from these women than he did working since the women were very grateful and more than willing to give him expensive gifts or invest money in his bogus schemes. He was very clever and moved around a lot so that he was gone before they realized what had happened. It was an easy way for him to get money and it was not a crime as much of what he received were gifts.

Mike liked a high lifestyle and despite all of the money he received, he was never able to save anything and was never anywhere long enough to purchase any real estate or investments. He also lived well and spent what he received on himself.

One of his potential victims was Maria who was a very attractive and wealthy widow visiting her uncle in the hospital. She lived alone in a very large and expensive house and worked part time as a hostess at a local very fine restaurant for something to do to keep her busy.

He was a gentleman and was always available to talk and spend a lot of time with her. He even helped her when she had to get her car serviced or with repairs around her house.

THE BOXES

Maria was small and dark, very well dressed, with expensive jewelry, and generous to him out of gratitude. She seemed to have few friends and had little contact with her family. She related to him that her husband had been a successful businessman and she made it clear to Mike that she wanted to be with him. All of these things made her a perfect mark and all he had to determine was how much he could get from her although she had already given him some very nice gifts.

Things were starting to get too close for Mike so he started talking to Maria about one of his allegedly successful but unfortunately bogus businesses for her to invest in. A large sum was discussed and she agreed to give him a large amount in cash which he told her had tax advantages. Mike could not believe how well he had handled this and how easy it was. However he had no idea how unfortunate his choice of a mark was. Mike arranged for Maria to meet him with the cash at a small out of the way restaurant. Things were going well and his plan was already in place for a rapid departure once he received the money.

He walked into the restaurant expecting to see Maria but instead there were three very large, muscular, burly men waiting for him and he knew immediately that he was in terrible trouble. He looked around, desperately looking for an escape route but the thugs were prepared and blocked the front and back exit.

One of the large men indicated for Mike to sit down at a table in the back and sat down across from him. The man did not introduce himself and said, "If you are waiting for Maria she's not coming."

Mike could only nod and was afraid to look at the men but a furtive glance at them told him they were not smiling. They were all well dressed in expensive suits. Mike wondered what he got himself into. He somehow knew that his avocation would someday get him into trouble and this was the day.

Mike was trembling and did not know what to expect when a smaller older man, also well dressed, with a black suit, shirt, and tie came in to the restaurant and sat down. One of the large men checked Mike to see if he had anything dangerous on his person.

The older man introduced himself, "I am Gino and unfortunately the lady you tried to con is related to someone you don't want to know. We had what you might call a conference and we figured out a way for you to do us a favor to make it up to us. If you agree we will let you live." He could tell that Mike seemed relieved that he was going to live and was not going to refuse.

Mike cleared his throat and said a feeble "Yes." This was not good and his imagination was far too prolific, thinking of what he had to do. Murdering someone came to his mind first.

Gino started talking. "First of all, you need a new name and history including documents and references. Working as a paramedic will get you to where we want you to be. There is a woman we want some documents from and we want to avoid suspicion or any connection to us. The lady will have an accident which she will survive and that is when you come on the scene doing what you do best. You will meet her and get close to her so that you can get us the documents." Gino needed to know what Alex did with the documents, her diary and incriminating photos, and if anyone else knew about them.

Mike was relieved, especially since he did not have to kill anyone. He said, "Alright. Where do I have to go and who is the lady?"

Gino continued, "We will let you know when the time comes. We know where you live and someone will be visiting you with everything you need. And don't think about trying to get away because if you try, we will find you and you will not be happy." Gino smiled, but it was not a happy smile.

Mike realized he was trapped and had no way out but to do what Gino said. What Gino said he had to did not sound all that difficult, especially with his skills. Mike did ask, "If I do this, will I have to worry about my safety?"

Gino said, "Just do what you are supposed to do and that relieves your obligation. However after this you have to give up taking advantage of ladies. "

Mike realized his profession of getting money from wealthy ladies was over and although he knew that it had been a good run. Now his life was at stake. He could do this.

With Gino's connections, Mike was hired as a paramedic at a local hospital. He was scheduled to work an evening when there was a call to go to the scene of an accident that involved two ladies that had been hit by a car. This was carefully arranged so that his ambulance arrived at the scene just after the accident. He suspected who was involved in causing the accident but he really did not want to know. He knew was that he was supposed to meet and get close to a lady doctor named Alex who he found out was one of the victims of the accident. The other lady Beth was hurt pretty badly but luckily she survived. Alex only had bruises and a few minor lacerations and by helping her at the hospital, they became friends. He visited her at the hospital and took her home after she was discharged after her hospitalization for observation for her concussion. It worked well and he was invited to her house for dinner. Everything had progressed smoothly as planned.

Alex showed him around her house when he took her home from the hospital he asked about the unopened boxes that he believed held what he needed to find. Unfortunately she refused to let him help her unpack them. She said the boxes contained mementos from the past in the boxes and she was not ready to open them.

Spending time at her house for a dinner invitation allowed him to disable her alarm and leave a window unlatched. Getting into her house would be easy while she was at work.

It took Mike a while to crawl into the laundry room through the window. He didn't want to alert her that the boxes had been opened or anything removed. As Alex sometimes came home for lunch he had to be judicious of his time in her house.

Mike remembered from when he was in Alex's house that all of the doors were locked with a key but Mike did not see the key anywhere. That meant that the window was his only access into or out of the house without breaking a window and searching for the key would have taken too much time. The last thing he wanted was to alert Alex that anyone had been there. He figured it would be simple to overlook an open window in the laundry room if nothing obvious was taken. Mike believed he could get himself invited back to the house some time where he could close and re-lock the window. It was a simple plan.

He was sure that he could open the boxes, remove what he was supposed to collect and close up the boxes so that no one could suspect that he had been there. Mike even purchased the same type of tape that Alex used so that he could reseal them. He was actually proud of himself for planning this so well.

Mike rented a car and exchanged the license plates on it with another similar car in a distant parking lot. He knew that most people don't notice for a while that they are driving their car with different license numbers as long as the plates look similar. He was making a very great effort to insure that he and his car were not identified by any witnesses so he parked the car he was driving two blocks away. Mike wore a uniform from an air conditioning company so that no one would pay any attention to him being around the house as long as no one noticed him going through the window. He had to wait until her neighbors left and the gardeners were working on the side of the house where they couldn't see him. Fortunately by the time he was ready to go in the gardeners had left.

When Mike climbed through the window he was careful to wipe his feet so that no dirt was tracked into the house or up the stairs. The house was empty and the boxes were in the same place in one of the bedrooms which almost seemed too easy. This pleased him thinking he would be off the hook with Gino soon. Mike leaned over and opened the first box but it held a bunch of junk, papers, napkins and the like, and the second box contained the same. Mike believed that what he needed must be in the third and last box. Unfortunately, the diary and the photo album were not there and in disbelief he turned the boxes upside down, spreading out the contents of the boxes on the floor. He was confused and upset because they had to be there! He turned on the light in the bedroom and looked through the closet but there was nothing there so he started looking through the rest of the house.

Mike did not expect to hear the doorbell ring and a knock on the door. Someone may have seen him enter the house and he did not know if the maids were coming in to clean. He cursed under his breath and panicked. The last thing he needed was to be found in Alex's house. He had no time go upstairs to replace everything strewn on the floor back into the boxes. Mike soundlessly moved to the laundry room and looked out the window to see if anyone was around. It was clear and he left through the window and unfortunately he had spent a lot longer than he planned in the house. He looked around and seeing no one watching, he walked unhurriedly to the rental car still hoping that no one would notice.

Mike now had to face Gino. He was still in disbelief that none of these boxes had the journal and photos he was supposed to get and now he was still in trouble. He wondered if there were boxes elsewhere that she did not tell him about or what if she had simply destroyed what he needed to find. However after seeing that the boxes contained all sorts of trashy mementos, he was pretty sure she would not have destroyed anything. However what he did see in the boxes confirmed that she was the person they were looking for.

When Mike called him to report that he did not get what he was supposed to, Gino told him to come by. Mike went in the back door of the bar where the matches came from that had been found on the floor of the car that had been used to harm Alex and Beth. Gino was seated at a table consuming a large plate of pasta waiting for Mike.

Mike was trying to hide his fear and Gino did not ask him to sit down which Mike knew was not a good sign. After a pause, Gino was not smiling and looked up at him. "What happened? The journal and photos were supposed to be in the boxes and you failed to find them." Gino looked at Mike coldly which sent a chill through him and then he started to sweat.

Mike was very nervous, because this was serious. "I did everything you told me to do and I looked through every box but they weren't there."

Gino thought carefully, "What if they are someplace else? I am giving you another chance to find them, and Alex must not be harmed. There was a history and a promise that protects her even now. She doesn't know what she has and she should never know so just find them."

Mike was only somewhat relieved when he left and he called Alex wanting to know if he could come over to her place that evening. She told him she was busy so he knew he would have to keep trying. He did not know how long he had.

This was very bad for him and he realized that all of the time, money, and effort for him to get close enough to Alex to get what was in the boxes, had been useless. His only chance was to be her friend to learn more, although she would be on alert after this break into her house. He had no choice but to try.

CHAPTER 28

BOXES AND CHANCE

The police station was still crowded and noisy when Chance left to go over to Alex's house. He wanted to talk about what was in the boxes that anyone else would want besides her. And of course Chance joked with himself about how he had to force himself to investigate this case with a beautiful woman and spend time with her to help her. It was a difficult job but he was always willing to help a person in need. At that point he was laughing at himself and he was actually elated to be going over to Alex's house. The night was stormy with a heavy downpour but that did not stop Chance from going there. Walking past his colleagues who were providing security outside of her house, they commented to him, "I wish I had your job." They smiled at each other.

Alex opened the door and after they greeted each other, he went into the house noticing the wonderful aroma of her food. Alex had made a roast with many side dishes for him for dinner and the food was excellent as well as the wine. They chatted pleasantly over dinner and laughed on occasion, trying to put off talking about anything serious.

After dinner Chance complemented Alex, "It was a wonderful meal and as good as I can remember but unfortunately you know this is not entirely a social call. Let's talk about the boxes that seem to have everyone's attention."

Alex started, "We talked about my relationship with Sal and the times we spent together on his yacht. We had a busy social life on his boat but I never paid attention to his many friends and business associates who came on board. We had been together over a year when one of his friends or maybe a business associate, asked me privately if I knew who Sal was. He was the first person to say anything to me about what Sal's business was, which wasn't important to me and I never asked him anything. This associate then told me that Sal was the head of a very large Italian family, a godfather. I always thought that a godfather was a character that was made up for the movies. He did have a lot of varied visitors to the boat but my contact with them was mostly limited to hanging out with their girlfriends or social pleasantries."

THE BOXES

Chance was silent now thinking of many questions he did not know how to ask. It was obvious that Alex had no idea what Sal was involved with which could have been a whole range of things and not all of them legal. He was now wondering what was in the boxes. He finally asked, "What do the boxes have to do with the time you spent with him?"

"Well, the time we were together was very special to me and I saved everything like clothing, napkins, post cards, matches and the like. Most of those were in the boxes here at my house."

"So what might be special about your mementos to anyone else?" Chance was very curious now, especially since he knew Sal was a major underworld figure.

"I can't imagine."

Chance smiled because he knew Alex was very intelligent but clueless about some things, this included. He said, "Enough suspense. Let's go look at the contents of your boxes."

Alex showed him around the house and they ended up in the bedroom that still had the papers and memorabilia strewn about the floor. Chance looked at all of the contents and didn't see anything special. He picked up a napkin, looked at it, and exclaimed, "This is it!!!! This is what all of the hoopla is about!!"

Alex looked at him holding this napkin and they both started laughing. He looked at everything on the floor and commented, "There is nothing here that is worth anything." He looked at her who had a hurt expression on her face and he tried to retract what he said, "Well except for memory value." This worked because she smiled. He continued, "Then I don't understand what they could have been looking for. Do you have any idea?"

Alex thought briefly and related, "I wanted to remember all of the time we were together, so I kept a diary of everything we did including the people I met although I only knew their first names. I also took a lot of photos of us on the boat."

Chance was starting to realize how important this could be. "Were the photos of just you and Sal or of anyone else?"

"There are a lot of pictures of us and others in the background."

Chance was silent, and then carefully asked, "Where are the pictures and diary now?"

"In the boxes I still have at Beth's."

Chance whistled. "I know who Sal was. So you are telling me that you have a record and photos of the people Sal associated with socially or for business? Were the photos pretty clear? "

"Yes. Sal bought me a new camera that registered the date they were taken and the pictures were pretty good. I didn't know who the people were and Sal kept some of the pictures although he did tell me to get rid of them, but he knew I still kept them. Sal and I had fun looking at them."

"Did anyone else see the pictures, like some of the people on his boat?" Chance was starting to understand the significance of what Alex had.

"Actually, Sal joked about them and we all had fun looking at the pictures."

Chance now realized the importance of the contents of the boxes and what some nefarious characters were looking for. The implications of photos of them taken on a boat with Sal could be monumental.

Alex continued, "I stored a lot of things at Beth's house when I moved in here as she had a lot more space. My other boxes are there and she would never throw them out.

Chance asked, "Can we go to Beth's house to see what you have?"

THE BOXES

Alex responded, "I am sure my boxes are there. I have a key to her house and Ben doesn't mind if I go over there. She still had some boxes of her's she also hasn't unpacked and I was helping her gradually go through her stuff."

Chance could barely control his excitement because this could explain a lot. "Do you realize that if something happened to you and no one knew what they were, the contents of those boxes would be unnoticed? Or if the contents of boxes just disappeared there would be no records of Sal's activities. You are the only one that knows where they came from. What does Beth know about Sal and the contents of the boxes?"

Alex replied, "She only knew that I was seeing someone and I never told her who Sal was or what's in any of the boxes."

Chance thought for a while and said to her, "It isn't too late. Let's go see the boxes."

Alex called Ben who was with Beth at the hospital and he told her it was no problem if she went to their house. Alex left the dishes in the sink and got her coat.

Beth's house was in a secure gated community and the house had a lot of alarms including cameras with motion detectors. Chance drove up to the house commenting, "I guess this could qualify as a mansion and it could take forever to find something. Are you sure you know where the boxes are?"

Alex laughed and replied, "Of course."

They went in, turned off all of the security devices and Alex took him to the back of the house. Chance incredulous, commented. "I don't think I even want to know how many bedrooms are in this house. I have never been in a house like this."

"It's comfortable." They both laughed.

Alex led him to one of the attached garages where the boxes were and Chance commented, "This is a garage? It does have a garage door but the floor has nice tile and it is air conditioned. This is a different life style and I can see why Ben was suspected of harming Beth. She obviously has a lot of money."

"But Ben would never harm her. He didn't know about what she had when he married her and they were living in his modest place until this place was built."

There was a lot of furniture in the garage and two walls of boxes, three deep. Alex easily found the three boxes they were looking for.

THE BOXES

Chance put one of the boxes on the desk and opened it and found only more mementos. He opened the second box and found the diary. He went through a number of pages and asked, "Are you sure you don't mind me going through this? It has quite a lot of information along with some pretty intimate details."

"I had nothing to hide. I wanted to remember everything." She smiled.

"I guess this diary could definitely allow you to remember everything!!!" They both laughed again.

The third and last box had a large album with many photographs with the dates they were taken and most were clear enough to see and identify the people in them. As Chance and Alex went through the photos she had no idea who they were. Several of the photos recorded envelopes passing from some visitors to Sal. Alex had assumed it was just papers which was part of a business deal so she never paid any attention to what they did.

Chance looked at her and said incredulously, "Do you have any idea what you have here? I can identify prominent businessmen, some senators and congressmen, a police commissioner, and some celebrities. One photo shows Senator Rushman giving Sal a thick envelope. The senator had no hope of winning his election until the person who was running against him died in a suspicious accident. I don't know when the accident happened but if this was close to this visit, there is no telling what arrangements were made." He continued. "I know this may be sensitive, but how did Sal die?"

"I heard he drowned but that didn't make sense to me. He was a good swimmer." Alex experienced some pain and regret but continued. "Sal knew about the diary because we often laughed at what I wrote and at the photos. I know a lot were pretty corny. I am pretty sure his visitors thought I was one of the bimbo girlfriends who was stupid like the others and would not remember anything. The girlfriends of his guests were certainly no mental giants. A few of Sal's companions knew I was a doctor but they did not pay any attention. It must have been suspicious when I moved and changed my name. A couple of the visitors noticed me taking photos but Sal told them not to worry. I am sure that he told them that the photos would disappear and some of them actually did. He even showed some of them to his friends for entertainment. However he did know I still had some and it told me not to worry about it and he even kept a few of the photos of us together. I put together this album after we separated."

"How would they know about the diary?"

"They probably saw me on the deck writing in it while they were discussing business."

Chance kept watching Alex who was trying to hide how upset she was and hoping he would not notice how much she was trembling. He asked her, "Are you ok?

"I am fine." Chance smiled at her to relieve some of her tension.

He continued, "I don't know for sure what happened but Sal ran with a tough crowd who knew about your photos and your diary. They don't know that you had no idea who they were when you documented a lot of the activities on Sal's boat. Obviously, what you have weren't with Sal's belongings except for the few photos he kept. They observed how close you and Sal were so they assumed you would not get rid of them. How am I doing so far?"

"Scaringly accurate." She seemed calmer.

"These photos and your knowledge are a powder keg and there is no way these people on the boat could ever allow anyone to find out about their association with Sal.

THE BOXES

Alex was stunned at first and could not say anything. Then she spoke. "What do we do?"

Chance was realistic because he knew that these photos were of wealthy, ruthless people that had a wide reaching influence including people at the police department who could get access to the evidence room there. He said, "We cannot take these to the police station because I would give them a very short life span before they magically disappeared. They seem safest here for now until I can figure out what agency to turn them over to. No one would suspect that they were here. Your police protection made sure we were not followed so the boxes are ok for now which brings us to you. After the bad guys had no success in finding this evidence, your life could be in danger. The people looking for this probably feel they can still get what you have."

Alex said, "Sal always told me he would protect me and never let anyone harm me."

"To simplify this, Sal obviously loved you and protected you by any means he had available while he was alive. Once he was gone they probably looked for the photos and diary in Sal's things and didn't find them. With him gone this evidence can't hurt him, but it could possibly implicate others and now you lost your protector."

Alex understood and realized just how much Sal had loved her. He had been protecting her all of this time, even after they were together.

While they were at the house Mike called wanting to see her. Chance told Alex, "I am wondering if Mike had anything to do with trying to get these documents. Once they were gone all that would be left is you and you did not know any of these guests of Sal's. There isn't anything that you could say that would be believable. You were committing adultery and hanging out with a notorious underworld figure which you wouldn't want made public since you are a respected member of the medical community. "

Alex nodded her head in agreement.

Chance suggested, "Let's put the diary and album into another container, perhaps one of Beth's boxes and reseal yours. We can take your boxes with only the mementos left to your house where you can get Mike to open them with you. He would think that what he was looking for was gone or destroyed. If he is involved, and it seems like he might be, that could reduce or eliminate the threat to you and give us some time to pursue this. Don't forget that you still have police protection which we are going to increase. What do you think?"

"That sounds good. I can't think right now but I am glad you are here."

"I am not telling anyone about this except Pete who will want to know and I don't know who else we can trust." Chance would have to determine what to do with the evidence.

Chance and Alex drove away from Beth's house taking a circuitous route so that it was not obvious where they were coming from. Chance walked Alex to her door where she lightly kissed him his on his cheek and waved at her police patrol. Chance waited while she took sandwiches, drinks, chips and fruit to her protectors who were very grateful. Chance admired her for taking care of the patrolmen and said goodnight.

Once she was home Alex, who had not known anything about what had happened with the car or the break in, was now afraid. There were some powerful people looking to get rid of what she had and possibly herself which made her sleep fitfully. This was not what she needed as she planned to go to work the next day.

THE BOXES

THE BOXES

CHAPTER 29

MIKE/BOXES LEAVE

Alex woke up even earlier than usual and watched the sun come up from her patio. The sky was clear with only a few wispy clouds and there was a gentle breeze. The flowers in her garden were blooming which gave a sweet scent to the air. She took time every day to be grateful for the wonderful things she had in her life including her health and a thriving medical practice. It was a glorious day and she took some coffee and sweet rolls out to her grateful security detail. She had a busy day scheduled in the office which she hoped would take her mind off of all of this.

On her way to the office, Alex thought about how difficult it would be for her to have Mike over to the house and especially if he might have had something to do with the break in. He seemed like a nice man and she had trouble believing that he was involved with the person or persons that tried to hurt her and Beth.

THE BOXES

Alex now believed that Beth was just an innocent victim when the car struck them. She talked to Beth frequently but she did not relate anything that was found out about the boxes or about Ben's female friend.

Alex went to see Beth at lunchtime and cheerfully greeted her. "Hi. How's the patient?"

Beth was happy to see her as usual. "I am fine and so ready to get out of here. I have been here so long I think they are going to name the room after me, Beth's abode." They both smiled. She continued, "But I have good news because maybe, and it is just maybe I might be able to go home in a week or two. Ben talked to my doctor about the possibility of getting a hospital bed in our house with a full time nurse but so far he wants me to stay until I get out of this large cast with this metal contraption."

"I am so excited for you but don't be disappointed if you can't leave yet. That is so nice of Ben to try to arrange that."

Beth became serious. "I suppose you know about what Livi did. I thought I knew her well after being friends for years but I guess I did not know her well enough. It makes more sense to me now that she abruptly wrote me out of her life. Ben hasn't talked about it as I think he was shocked and badly hurt by her actions. This is difficult for both of us to understand and accept what she did. Well enough of this and tell me what is happening in your life? What about the tall good looking fellow that visits me sometimes and seems very fond of you?"

Alex thought about this being a bad time to discuss Mike who could be involved with some nefarious people and activities that involved the two of them being injured, but she had to be upbeat. She thought about how he was probably involved in the break in, but she said, "Fine. We talked some and have been out to eat a few times but we are not together." Alex managed an insincere smile and added, "I really didn't know Livi that well and I was surprised that anyone could do something like this to you especially. I feel badly for Ben as he had been a good friend to Livi for a long time. A friend or even a decent person does not try to seriously harm anyone."

Beth commented, "I realize that and I am sad that Ben was so badly hurt but at least things are good with us. We are lucky to have each other."

"I am just glad that things worked out between you and let me know if you can go home. Love you."

Alex thought about her situation. Yes I am fine too, considering I had an affair with a married underworld crime figure and now I am having repercussions from that including my life being in danger. She laughed which was better than crying.

Alex said goodbye to Beth and called Mike. Chance connected her to a three way conversation when she called him. Alex asked Mike, "Hi, how have you been?"

"Great and even better hearing from you."

Alex tried not to seem as nervous as she felt and said, "I am trying to catch up with a lot of paperwork around here and I would like your help if you have time. I have a light bulb that needs changing and I found some more of those old storage boxes here that I need to sort out. I thought you could help since you were nice enough to offer to help with the other ones." She kept reminding herself that there would be a police detail at and around and at her house when he was there which made her feel only somewhat better.

"No problem and when should I come over?"

"Do you have any time today maybe at after work?"

"I will be there and you need me to bring anything?"

Alex thought, no weapons please, and answered, "No, just yourself."

Alex and Mike hung up and Chance called her, "Are you sure you are ok with this?" He knew she was nervous.

"Just dandy." and she laughed nervously. "I don't practice high adrenaline medicine but I guess I signed up for this because I know it is the right thing to do. I do appreciate your help with all of this and is this how Mata Hari felt?"

He laughed. "Don't worry. I will be around and you will have a lot of protection."

Mike was relieved when he heard there were more boxes and he was optimistic thinking hopefully they contained what Gino wanted. He immediately called Gino.

"I wanted you to know that I am going to her house tonight to help her unpack some other boxes. I went through all of the boxes at her house before but I didn't find any others when I searched the house. Now she said there are more boxes which must have been someplace else but they are at her home now.

Gino was pleased and relieved thinking it was time to finish this. He reminded Mike, "You know what will happen if you fail again. Do whatever you have to do to finish this and I mean anything."

Mike understood the extent he had to go to if necessary but he did not panic. This was a long way from just romancing women for money but unfortunately he had been caught by the worst people possible. He was hoping this would be easy. And even though Alex was smart he thought that maybe she really did not know the incriminating things she had in her possession. Hopefully she just thought they were memorabilia and did not remember much. People keep things to remember good times but what if she knew too much? This could become a very sticky and lethal situation which he wanted no part of because this was a bad bunch he was involved with. He looked at the large razor sharp knife that Gino had given him and knew he could never use it.

Alex was impressed at the preparations that were made at her house for Mike's visit, noting that the police had officers that were going to be hidden in her house, in her garage, and even the closet for when Mike came over. They instructed her to put a few loose things in front of the closet door where they were to make it look like it hadn't been used in a while. They also placed multiple cameras and recording devices around.

It was seven pm when Mike was due and Alex was very nervous but she felt as ready as she could be. She was ready for this to be over. Mike arrived and she kissed him on the cheek as usual so that he would not think there was anything wrong. "Hello and thanks for coming over. Have you been busy?"

"Nothing special, the same old things."

"Would you like some wine?" And Alex was thinking, 'I could use a couple of shots of liquor.'

He agreed and she poured a couple of glasses. She suggested, "Why don't we take the glasses upstairs and get to work." She wanted him there for as short a time as possible and she managed a smile.

In the back bedroom the boxes that had already been opened were gone with only a few things left that Alex kept which were now stored in a small plastic container. The three boxes that had been at Beth's house which Alex and Chance had already gone through, no longer contained the diary or photos. They were carefully resealed so they looked like they had never been opened. Alex and Mike opened them and laid out the contents which had only papers with other memorabilia. Mike looked at everything carefully. Alex could tell he was very anxious and asked him, "Is everything alright? This is just meaningless stuff except to me, of course." And she smiled, a real smile this time.

Mike looked at Alex and asked, "Are these all of the boxes? If there are more I am willing to help."

Alex was nervous and trying to appear calm said, "Yes. I had these in another closet (or maybe a garage she thought) and I am glad to get rid of a lot of stuff I do not need."

Mike could tell she wasn't telling the truth because when he had broken into her house and did not find what he was looking for in the boxes he had searched her house thoroughly. He went through her desk, file cabinets, closets and drawers, even looking for a record of her having a storage unit but found none. These boxes had been someplace else obviously. Now he questioned if she knew the importance of the diary and photos and had removed them or if there were just more boxes in the same place she got these. Mike tried to hide his distress realizing he had to face Gino and did not know what to say. He did everything he could but he failed, again. He wasn't good at this and now he again had to tell Gino that he didn't have what he was supposed to find. His phone was downstairs and he had to leave to make the call.

Hiding his devastation, he said, "I am glad I helped you but unfortunately I have to go because I am working early in the morning."

"Thanks for coming over to help and have a good evening." which she knew he wouldn't. He walked out seeming to be in a hurry. She was relieved that this part was over.

As soon as Mike left he called Gino on the way to his car and he didn't notice that he was observed by the policeman and Chance who were watching the house. They had no proof to arrest him or question him so they had to let him drive away.

All of the officers and Chance came out of their hiding places and Alex breathed a sigh of relief. Chance smiled and commented. "You were great! Maybe you could change your profession and become a spy? We could use a femme fatale on the force."

Alex gave him a look like she could hurt him and then started laughing, joined in by everyone. Hopefully they accomplished what they planned.

THE BOXES

Mike's conversation with Gino was not a good one. He said he didn't think Alex was telling him the truth about the whereabouts or of the contents of these boxes. Gino was upset and had some choice words with Mike. "You failed and it seems that this Alex broad is hiding something and we need to know what she knows, where she has the diary and more. Do you think she suspected that you broke in and was trying to get us off the track by showing you some useless boxes?"

"I am not sure because I was very careful and she cannot prove anything."

Gino thought for a while, then continued, "Does this broad know anything and is she working with anyone?"

Gino's thoughts did not surprise Mike. "I don't know." although he believed she lied to him.

"Ok. Go home and we will handle it from here." Gino had already researched Alex and knew where she lived and worked. It was time to contact his police connections that were on his payroll.

Mike rushed to where he was staying, collected some belongings and left in his car. He didn't know what Gino was going to do to him and although he hoped Gino would just let him go, he couldn't take that chance. He never did get money from his mark but the threat to him was more than enough to get him to do what he had to, but he failed several times. He was frightened and drove away not caring where he went as long as it was far, knowing he had to disappear.

The ATM that he stopped at gave him what little money he had left in the bank and he threw out all of his credit cards so that he could not be traced. He kept thinking about what a bad situation he had gotten himself into. He was not a paramedic but Gino had gotten him the right paperwork to get the job at the hospital and luckily Mike had enough medical experience so he was able to manage it. He had to go far away to be able survive somehow. He cancelled his cell phone service, destroyed his phone and left the pieces in a trash container. His final act was going to an airport in a distant city and leaving his car there after he had wiped it down to remove his fingerprints. A shuttle took him to a bus station where he caught a bus to wherever it was going.

Actually, Gino figured that Mike was on the run but he didn't care since Mike failed. Gino had no reason to pursue him. Mike would be long gone and would never tell anyone what was going on even though he knew too little anyway.

Gino called Mike's cell phone and found that the service was discontinued. He knew Mike was gone. Gino did chuckle at the punishment that Mike suffered by having to do all of these things was deserved, and he was certain that Mike was done with his gigolo days. Gino laughed at this for a while although he now had to accomplish what he had been well paid for.

CHAPTER 30

ALEX AND THE MOB

Gino now had to find the photos and diary himself and he called several of his contacts he had at the police department. He was told that Alex was under a protective detail and there were even policemen at her house but they didn't know why. The request had made by one of their detectives and Gino now realized this was worse than he thought.

Gino called his connections, "Was anything turned into the department like any papers or photos?

His contact replied. "There wasn't anything turned in."

Gino was relieved but now knew with Alex and the documents gone it was only hearsay and now it was time to talk to Alex. He was being paid a very large sum to take care of this and he also knew that with Mike gone, there was no connection to him or his client. He figured that this police detective seemed pretty clever and was probably the one that had Mike come to the house. It also made sense that if the documents were around, the detective would not keep them at his place since they could be found too easily. Wherever the additional boxes or what he needed were unknown.

What Gino had to do was simple. He had a lot of paid people at the police station and removing the protection from this lady would be easy. The reason they were protecting her was nebulous to them and he did not want anything to happen to this detective. Harming someone in the police department would warrant too many repercussions.

Chance had an idea that whomever was after the boxes had police connections that would make sure that any evidence turned in there from Alex would disappear. He had no doubt that Alex was in danger. He needed some outside help and a trustworthy friend directed him to a high ranking FBI agent, Matthew, that he was told is a straight shooter. Chance met with him and described all that had happened along with what the diary and photos were in detail. Chance said he was afraid to remove the documents from their hiding place and Matthew agreed.

Matthew was the assistant director of the FBI and told Sal, "We know well who Sal was and about many of his, we'll let us say associates. We have been doing an extensive investigation of his activities and found only minor things but nothing that we can use. We suspected a number of things but we could not do anything without proof."

Chance related, "Several years ago Alex spent a lot time with Sal and kept a lot of mementos including a diary and dated photographs of him and his associates while they were on his yacht."

Matthew thought about this and looked at Chance, "This is a powder keg. Where is Alex now? "

"She is probably at her office but we have protection for her both at her office and at home. No one questioned why and fortunately it helps to be on the force."

Chance called Sheila who was in charge of the security detail to check on Alex, "How is it going?"

Shelia was surprised. "I guess no one called you. The security was called off this morning."

Chance was upset and knew how that happened. "Thanks. I will get back to you." He looked at Matthew and anxiously said, "Someone in the department called off Alex's protection this morning."

Matthew was stoic and asked, "Where is Alex's office?"

Chance gave him the details including a description of her car.

Matthew made a call. "We are sending men there now because she needs to be in protective custody with us now. There is obviously some questionable stuff going on at your police station."

Chance rushed over to her office as well, knowing that Alex would be leaving the office to have lunch shortly.

Chance and two cars with FBI agents were driving up to Alex's office just as two large men forced her into a dark car and drove away. Chance jumped into one of the agent's cars and announced, "I am going with you."

Matthew nodded his head and called Chance's superior at the station. He explained, "Chance is needed to cooperate and work with the FBI in this assignment. He has necessary information for the solution to this situation." Chance's superior agreed.

Matthew next called his captain to explain the necessity of including Chance in the operation. He told him, "Chance's official cooperation is an essential part for the rescue of a lady who had evidence of the involvement and possible crimes of a known underworld figure which may also include a number of public figures."

Matthew's captain agreed and said be careful. "If you need any additional help, let me know."

Matthew added, "Not right now since we already have a number of agents to help but we will let you know if that changes."

Their cars discretely followed the vehicle that Alex was in trying not to alert the men inside. Matthew could tell that Chance was agitated but he was hiding it pretty well. Matthew said, "They are not going to harm her until they get to wherever they are going. These are probably henchmen and we need to get who is doing this. They will lead us there. Don't worry because we have a number of cars in the area now and we won't lose them. We also have a helicopter coming that will discretely pass over so they won't realize they are being observed. Obviously they need the documents also and otherwise something would have happened to Alex sooner."

Chance was feeling only somewhat better and became intent on the chase.

The dark car was not speeding to avoid attention and followed a route to an isolated building by the airport.

THE BOXES

There were already some cars there including one with a government license. Matthew commented, "Interesting mix of cars. We have to defuse this situation, get inside, and keep Alex from being harmed." He made it sound easy and believable but he was still concerned about an innocent person.

Alex was sitting between the large men that forced her into the dark car. She was frightened and trembling. "I can give you money. Let me go." She was near tears.

The three men in the car did not say anything and she wondered where the police were that were protecting her. She was ushered into a building where she heard airplanes and seated in a chair where her hands were tied. Alex had no idea where she was except that there were no lights or other buildings around with only a dirt road leading there. She was certain that no one would ever find her there and that she had no chance of survival.

Gino walked over to her, leaned over, and said, "You know what we want and you can make this easy on yourself. We will do what is necessary to get the information. Where are the journal and the photos?"

Alex looked up at the rough men who showed no emotion, "I don't have them." She was shaking. She was certain that once they got them she would be eliminated.

Gino looked at the men standing around him and said to Alex, "You will tell us what we want to know and Mario here is very good at getting people to talk. You are a very beautiful woman and it is a shame to change that." Mario moved to stand next to Gino who said with a smile, "I will be upstairs." And he looked at Mario, "Do what you need to do."

Mario struck Alex hard on her cheek and she started to cry. She knew her life was over.

Matthew had six men with him plus Chance and motioned towards the building, "There are no windows in the front so let's take a look around the back." Surveillance of the building showed that it was old wood structure and Matthew knew that the only way in was through the front or through the walls. There was a very muscular man standing in front of the door who was heavily armed. One of the FBI agents pulled out a thermal imaging device and circled around to the back with a few agents. Chance followed him, impressed with the equipment they had. The device worked well and Matthew indicated that there were four people on the main floor and two people in what looked like a loft. They could tell that on the main floor there were three people standing and one was seated. The three people downstairs that were standing had dense objects that Matthew indicated could be large weapons and one of the two people upstairs had what could be a small weapon.

Matthew and the agents went back to their cars and pulled out some heavy artillery along with some protective vests including one for Chance.

Chance asked, trying not to appear too anxious, "How are we going to get Alex out?"

Mathew smiled and said, "It looks like time for the delivery guy." Chance looked at him while the others chuckled.

Matthew indicated to one of the men as he pulled out some shorts and a shirt and put them on over his vest. The shirt said 'Luigi's Pizza' and he pulled out a pizza box. Chance was surprised when he saw this. He asked Matthew, "Does this really work?"

Mathew looked at him and said, "Unless you have another suggestion......"

"Just tell me what to do. I am ready."

The agent with the pizza box sauntered up to the burly man standing in front of the building and said "Pizza delivery."

The man in front of the building looked at him. "Go away. No one ordered pizza."

The agent posing as a delivery person scratched his head while looking at a piece of paper and said, "Yep, this is the address. Somebody ordered pizza."

Confused, the man in front opened the door and called in, "Did anyone order pizza?"

Gino had just walked upstairs and heard the shout about pizza. He yelled down, "You idiots! What are you doing?"

The FBI agents took advantage of the open door and quickly knocked out the outside guard. They rushed in and shot out the lights inside and the three men downstairs started shooting. One man was killed when the agents returned fire and the remaining men crouched down and were still shooting. Right at that time, three of the agents with Chance came crashing through the back wall. Chance rushed over to Alex and pulled her chair over to keep her out of the line of fire. The last two men downstairs started shooting wildly and the FBI agents shot them. The altercation happened very quickly.

Gino rushed down the stairs with his gun drawn and started shooting, striking Chance in his arm. Gino was shot by several of the agents who were crouched on the floor. The agents rushed upstairs where they found Senator Rushman pacing and saying'" I had nothing to do with this. I am a United States senator." He didn't know what to say and kept repeating it although he knew it was hopeless to try to claim innocence.

Alex was next to Chance who ignored his injury when he untied her. She had bruises and scrapes including a large bruise on her face but she was able to move. He said, "Thank goodness you are all right."

Although Alex was hurt and terrified, she said to Chance, "I know you always wanted to push me around." She looked at Chance who was smiling at her remark. She saw the blood coming from his arm and exclaimed, "Oh no! You are hurt. Are you alright?"

Chance looked at his arm which he had difficulty moving and answered lightly, "I guess I have been better." His arm was bleeding profusely and he sat down. Matthew took off his necktie and tied it around Chance's arm and

Chance looked at him and commented, "Who wears a tie to a gunfight?"

Matthew chuckled, and said, "Well after all, we are the FBI."

That made Chance really laugh, and he said, "Ouch. It hurts when I laugh" but he still continued. "Thanks."

Senator Rushman realized that he was caught in a criminal act and he had no chance of getting out of this. With Alex alive to testify about the journal and the photos he knew he would be convicted for his part in her kidnapping as well as for arranging the death of his political opponent when he was running for office. His records would show the money that he took out of his campaign fund to have his opponent eliminated. Now he was involved in this arrangement to get rid of Alex and the evidence. The payoff money to Gino was upstairs and the senator knew that his life was over. He thought about what would happen to his wife and children when all of this came out. There was only one way to protect them.

As the senator was being led downstairs by one of the agents, he spotted Gino's gun on the floor and pretended to trip and fall. He grabbed the gun before anyone could stop him and he shot himself in the mouth. He died quickly.

Alex was shocked. The agents had seen a lot of terrible things so they just acknowledged it.

Alex was holding Chance and told him, "We should call you an ambulance."

Chance looked at Alex and said, "Ok, I am an ambulance." He gave her a mischievous smile. He added, "I don't need an ambulance. It's not that bad." Alex realized that they were on an unmarked road far from anything and it would take a long time for an ambulance to find them.

Alex looked at the blood, trying to sound calm and said, "We really need an ambulance or any way to get him to the hospital quickly." She looked at Chance, then Matthew and muttered something under her breath to herself. Chance didn't hear her but Matthew caught a small part of what she said. He heard 'macho' and 'testosterone'. He smiled and looked at Alex while trying not to laugh. He knew then that Alex was all right because she still had her sense of humor.

Alex realized that they couldn't wait on an ambulance so Matthew and one of the agents helped Chance into a police car. Another agent commented, "It looks pretty rough inside the building. We are collecting evidence and we already called the coroner so I will finish up in here.

Your next stop is the hospital." He looked at Alex and said to Chance "You are in good hands."

Looking at the blood seeping from Chance's arm, Matthew told the agent driving, "Don't waste any time. Use your lights and siren." Chance was put in the back seat in a reclining position over Alex's lap and she was concerned about him going into shock.

Alex kept Chance talking to keep him awake. She looked at the screen separating them from the front seat of the car and remarked, "Since we are in the back seat of a police car behind the screen where people who are arrested sit, does that make us criminals?"

Chance laughed out loud and replied, "If you can't do the time, don't do the crime." Alex, Chance and the two agents in the car chuckled. Alex was happy that Chance was still awake and could still joke even in this serious situation.

Alex retorted, "I guess this means that since I am in the back of a police car and when someone says they saw me before, I can tell them they probably saw my picture with a number under my face on the post office wall for the most wanted criminals." They all laughed.

Chance commented, "I never thought that getting injured could be so much fun."

Alex added, "And now you will be tended to by gorgeous nurses." Chance smiled.

Alex was happy that the hospital they were going to was an excellent facility and the doctors there were very competent. She was grateful to Chance for everything he did to help her and he was a friend. She was going to be there to help him.

CHAPTER 31

CHANCE TO HOSPITAL

Alex, Chance and some agents were on the way to the hospital and their flashing lights and sirens got them easily through the heavy traffic. Some of the agents stayed at the building to take care of the carnage with police forensics agents along with waiting for the coroner to transport the bodies.

Sitting in the back seat of the car with Chance, Alex felt as though it was a taking a long time to get to the hospital although they arrived there quickly. Chance's legs were elevated to try to keep his blood pressure stable to avoid him going into shock. The necktie tourniquet was slowing the circulation to Chance's arm to reduce the bleeding but he was very pale from his blood loss. Alex could tell the bone in his upper arm was badly broken and with that much bleeding he needed surgery soon. Chance did not complain although Alex could tell that he was very uncomfortable, trying to shift around to get into a better position.

Alex called the emergency room and there was an emergency team with a cart ready for them when they pulled up. Chance was moved onto the cart and an IV was started and fluids were already running in the few short minutes it took to get Chance inside the emergency room. Alex followed Chance and the team inside. Chance looked at Alex and commented, "There is nothing like some VIP service."

The nurses moved quickly, checking his vitals and his arm and removed his clothing while being careful to avoid releasing the necktie that was tied around his arm. They were also concerned at his pallor and fearful of his going into shock. They were drawing blood just as Doctor Katz came in and he started checking Chance. When he noticed Alex he chuckled and commented to her, "You don't seem to be able to stay away from the emergency room." And when he saw the bruise on Alex's face he told a nurse to get some ice for her. He asked Chance "What happened?"

Chance was now somewhat obtunded and answered feebly, "Gunshot." Dr Katz Looked at Chance, ordered X-rays, checked his blood oxygen and he made a cursory exam of Chance's hand and arm. The surgeon, Dr Franklin who was on call and a friend of Alex's, walked in at that moment. Alex had called him while they were on the way and they were ready for Chance in the operating room. Dr. Franklin explained to Chance, "We are taking you to surgery and you need a blood transfusion because it looks like you lost a lot of blood. You have a pretty bad fracture of your arm and you need surgery to fix it including needing repairs to some of your blood vessels. Don't worry. You are in good hands.

All of the consent forms were signed and they started infusing the blood that he was typed for on the way to the operating room. Alex called Pete to tell him that they were in the hospital and briefly explained what had happened. Pete asked if she was alright and before she could answer, he said, "I will be right over."

As Chance was being taken away into the operating room, Dr. Katz pulled Alex aside and sat her down where they checked her vitals. He joked, "Unlike the last time you were here in the hospital I don't want you to wait until someone finds you in the waiting room and brings you be checked." Alex managed a smile. He asked, "You look pretty ruffled and are you alright?"

She answered, "I am but I'm more worried about Chance."

He told her although she already knew, "He will be in surgery for hours and you need to take care of yourself. You are getting checked out here and then you can wait but you really should consider going home to get some rest." Even as he mentioned that he knew she was going to stay.

After Alex was checked and cleared she went to the waiting room by the surgical department. She joked to herself that she may be a doctor but she could not handle watching Chance have surgery. Alex looked at her blood stained clothing and laughed thinking, 'I can't seem to be able to get away from being all bloody and here I am in the waiting room looking like I lost the fight.'

Matthew walked in and looked at her, "You look rough but are you alright?"

"I am, thanks. You really know how to complement a girl," and she managed a weak smile. She went on, "the injury to his arm was pretty severe and we had to call in a vascular surgeon also."

"How long will he be in surgery?"

Alex took a deep breath and answered, "I am not sure but it will be hours."

"Can I make a suggestion? Why don't I take you to your place where you can clean up and we can stop on the way back to pick up your documents that all of this hoopla was about?"

Alex wasn't thinking clearly but when she looked down at herself she realized she did look pretty bad so she agreed, "Sure."

Fortunately her house and Beth's were not far from the hospital and they started at her house first. Mathew said he had paperwork to do and some calls to make so he did not mind waiting for Alex. Alex directed him to the kitchen and told him to help himself to anything there and to make himself at home. It did not take Alex long to shower, wash her hair, and put on some jeans. This was a relief. She felt like she was washing away many of her troubles although she was very concerned about Chance. His injury was not life threatening but it was pretty severe.

Matthew was waiting patiently and commented, "This is a lovely house, very comfortable."

"Thanks."

As they left Alex's house, Matthew asked, "So where are we going?"

THE BOXES

Alex called Ben to tell him that she needed to pick up some things at his house and he said it was never a problem. She did not want to go into detail just then about what happened because she didn't want him or Beth to worry.

Matthew and Alex went to Beth's house and retrieved the diary and the photo album from the box where she and Chance had them stored.

Matthew looked at all of the other boxes in the room and commented, "It would take anyone else days to look through all of these boxes. Are a lot of them yours? This is a great choice for a hiding place, sort of like hiding a tree in a forest." They both laughed.

They returned to the surgery waiting room and were told that Chance was still in surgery.

One of the FBI agents came in as well, concerned about Chance and to help with the documents. Matthew sat next to her and asked, "Do we have your permission to look at the diary and photos?"

Alex agreed, "We will be here for a while anyway but I want you to know that this diary is a very personal thing that I wrote in, and it was never meant for public view."

Matthew and the other agent agreed, "Don't worry. We are treating this as personal and private and only the pertinent information will even be used."

Alex was relieved, "Thanks. I appreciate that."

Alex's office manager Cassie had called her repeatedly when Alex did not come back to the office from lunch. She was worried about her boss because Alex never missed office hours without calling to cancel and reschedule the patients. Cassie didn't see Alex being pulled into the dark car when she left for lunch. Cassie had seen the police cars around the office but she felt uncomfortable talking to her boss about it. She imagined a lot of explanations of why the police were there and although she had worked for Alex since she opened her office, she was more than an employee. They were friends also. Alex often took her employees to lunch or some medical meetings in nice places and her employees willingly worked very hard knowing that they were appreciated. They all worked well together and the office ran very smoothly. Finally Alex answered and told Cassie, "I am alright now, even though I was kidnapped by some bad people and rescued by the police with the FBI. It was a tough day." She laughed at how matter of factly she described her terrible experience.

Cassie was shocked, and said, "Wait a minute. Did you just say what I thought you did?"

"Unfortunately, yes."

Cassie now wide-eyed with disbelief continued, "I can't believe what happened and are you sure you are ok? Where are you and do you need anything or for me to come over?" She was rambling and still trying to process what she had heard.

Alex was grateful to have such a good friend and she replied, "I am alright and I don't need anything right now except that I am going to take a break and please cancel my patients for a week. My friend Chance was shot when I was being rescued and I am at the hospital waiting for him to come out of surgery."

Cassie gasped and said, "Shot? Do you mean from gunfire? You were in a place where people were getting shot? "

Alex started chuckling to herself at her comments. "Yes I was there but I am fine now." Alex thought, well as fine as I could be with a near death experience where people were killed or injured, complete with the suicide of a bad guy. She thought that it was pretty upsetting but she did not have the time for it to affect her and she could fall apart later.

Cassie asked, "Do you need a change of clothes or anything?"

Alex replied, "I was able to change into fresh clothes so I am all right for now. I am sorry I didn't call you earlier to report. Thanks for the offer and I will keep you posted as far as what is going on. I am calling Dr Fred to ask him to cover for me for a week. And I would appreciate your not telling anyone about this so just say I am taking a sort of vacation." She chuckled again. She thought, 'I guess this is what I have to do to give myself some time off.' She tried to make herself comfortable in in the waiting room, knowing she would be there for a while.

The hours that Chance was in surgery were difficult for Alex and although she knew he would come through easily and the extent of damage to his arm was to be determined. The vascular surgeon found extensive damage in addition to his bad fracture.

Alex was in the waiting room when Cassie came in carrying a large picnic basket of food for her. Cassie knew that Alex would stay in the waiting room to hear news about Chance. Cassie could tell how stressed Alex was and said, "Boss, you have to eat something because you are looking a little haggard and you don't have any weight to lose."

Alex smiled at her and said, "Thanks, mom." This made them both laugh. Alex did manage to eat some of the delicious food that Cassie brought and they sat for a while. Alex finally said, "Cassie you are the greatest and I appreciate all of this but I am good now. You need to go home to your family."

Cassie smiled and said, "All right but take care of yourself. I am available any time you need anything since my boss decided to take the week off so I have lots of time."

This made Alex laugh again and she said, "Good try." Cassie was pleased to see Alex laughing, especially since when she got to the waiting room Alex was pale and she could tell rattled. Cassie knew she did a good deed by coming and she really cared about her employer and friend. Cassie left insisting that Alex keep the basket of food which had enough food for a week, while Alex returned to her vigil.

THE BOXES

Pete arrived, short of breath from hurrying to the hospital and said, "I came as fast as I could. How are you and how is Chance?"

Alex looked at his red face and said, "Relax because Chance will be in surgery for a while and he is in good hands. Are you alright?"

Pete said, "I am as good as I can be after finding out that you were kidnapped and my beloved nephew has been injured and is in surgery. How long will Chance be in surgery?"

Alex replied, "I don't know and Cassie brought a basket of her wonderful cooking. We will be here a while so you may as well enjoy some of the goodies."

"You have been through a very traumatic experience and how are you holding up?"

Alex replied, "I am as good as can be expected but what happened hasn't hit me yet. There is nothing like worrying about a friend to make you forget your problems." She mustered a smile and hugged him. "I am glad you are here. Chance had a lot of damage to his arm but we won't know the full extent for a while."

Pete commented, "Well I am here now for both of you and you know that the two of you are my two most favorite people in the world." He looked in the basket and whistled, "This is quite a lot of good food and I don't mind partaking in some of it."

The surgery took six hours and by then Alex was emotionally as well as physically depleted. Between her ordeal and the injury to her good friend and savior, Chance, she was numb but still patiently waiting. She was grateful that Pete was here.

The surgeon, Dr Franklin came out, introduced himself to Pete and told them, "Chance is in the recovery room and he is good except that he had a severe injury to his arm. His humerus was shattered and there was some damage to his nerves and vessels. We repaired the damage as well as we could but we don't know how much function he will regain in his arm. This will be difficult for him as he is right handed. He will require a lot of therapy and emotional support."

Pete looked at the doctor and said, "Thank you doctor. Is he awake? When can we see him?"

Dr Franklin replied, "It won't be long since he will be in the recovery room shortly." He looked at Alex with the bruise on her cheek looking pale and disheveled. "How are you doing?"

Alex smiled and said, "I am fine and thanks for your help. How long will Chance be in the hospital?"

Dr. Franklin responded, "He will be here for a while since we had to do external fixation to his arm plus the extensive repair to his blood vessels. He will have a lot of pain."

Pete and Alex smiled at each other knowing Chance wouldn't let pain bother him and would try to tough it out with very little medication.

Dr Franklin said, "If you have any questions call me. I will be back in the morning." Alex and Pete didn't have to express how very worried they were about Chance but were thankful he survived

CHAPTER 32

ARM TREATMENT-AFTER SURGERY

Pete and Alex were chatting in the waiting room when a nurse from the surgery suite came out and told them that Chance was in the recovery room. She told them, "He is awake but still sleepy from the anesthetic and you can go in to see him but only briefly."

Alex looked at Pete and noticed that he was tired and pale from all of this stress although still managing to hold up. She knew she was stressed and fatigued as well but she overlooked it worrying about Chance. If he lost function in his arm from the injury this would interfere with his ability to be a police detective. She tried not to think about how much this would affect him but she would help him in any way she could. This had been a very long day and she was thankful that she was taking the week off. She still hadn't allowed herself to process what had happened that day. She knew that adrenaline kicks in when something like this happens and she knew she was amped up from it. She was going to crash mentally and physically as soon as she had a break but she had to be there for Chance. Pete were going to help him for whatever he needed.

They were finally ushered into the recovery room and although Alex knew that Chance would be bandaged, she did not imagine the massive dressings and bandages that had been placed on his arm. His arm had pins in it piercing the skin to keep the bones in place and he had a large splint on his arm under the bandages. His arm was suspended from a metal rod over his bed and his hand was very bruised and swollen. She already knew that this was a serious injury and the rehabilitation was going to be lengthy but seeing all of this made her realize how bad it was.

Alex said to Chance, "Hello and how are you feeling?"

Chance answered feebly, "Good, considering." And he looked at his arm." He continued, "This is quite a contraption. Did they have to bring in a mechanical engineer to put this together?" He smiled. His speech was a little slurred from the anesthesia but at least his spirits seemed good.

Pete joined in, "You are looking good." He was trying to cheer Chance up.

Chance smiled and at Pete's remark, "You never could lie well. I am pretty sleepy with the drugs and all and the nurse told me I was in surgery a long time. At least I was asleep but you two weren't so you should go home and get some rest. If you don't leave you will both be in bad shape and not worth anything. Don't worry. I am receiving excellent treatment."

Before Alex and Pete could say anything else, the nurse told them, "We are taking him to the intensive care unit because we have to closely monitor him. There is nothing you can do now but get in the way so the two of you should go home to get some rest." She smiled at them and turned to Chance to check the pulse oximeter on his finger which monitored his pulse and oxygen level. She was pleased with the reading.

Alex said to the nurse, "We are going home and here are our phone numbers. If anything happens, please call us. We will be back in the morning."

On their way out Matthew stopped Alex in the hall and said to her, "When you wake up tomorrow morning and only if you feel like it, can I come by to go over your documents and photos?"

Alex agreed and they left. Pete told her to call him when she got home and when she woke up so that they could get her car the next day from her office. When Pete dropped her off at her house her car was in the driveway which Alex knew was the work of her wonderful friend Cassie. She knew she was very lucky to have her and how thoughtful Cassie had been, bringing her the basket of food. Cassie was a very good friend.

Alex was very happy to be home but now she had no distractions to keep her from thinking about what she had been through, the accident, the concussion, Beth's injuries, her kidnapping and Chance's injury. She thought she would have trouble sleeping even though she was exhausted. She called Beth to check on her but couldn't mention what happened because Beth needed to heal and not worry about anything. Alex placed her cell phone next to her bed and when she laid down she fell immediately to sleep.

It was mid-morning before Alex woke up and she bolted upright, at first not realizing where she was but relieved to be in her own bedroom. The sun was streaming in and what had happened the day before seemed like a bad dream. She checked her phone and was glad there were no calls which meant there were no emergencies. The first thing she did was to call the hospital to check on Chance who was reported to be doing well. Alex was in no hurry to call Matthew because she wasn't ready to discuss anything yet, especially the diary and boxes.

Alex's cheek was swollen and very tender which brought back the memory of having been tied to a chair and struck in the face. The fear that she was going to die the night before came too clearly to her mind. Getting past this was going to be more difficult than she thought and her anxiety was high even though it was over. She hoped she would not have a post-traumatic stress disorder that often came from a stressful and frightening experience. PTSD could be severe and have a very negative effect on her life or anyone's and this was the last thing she needed. She wasn't hungry but she knew she had to eat something, at least a protein shake. She did not know what to do now especially since she could not focus on anything.

Being a physician she knew that she needed to see a psychologist to talk to and work things out. The people that try to tough it out and not seek professional help often had the worst problems getting over terrible experiences. She was on the other side now, a patient instead of a doctor and if any of her patients had experienced something like this, she would advise them to see a psychologist or psychiatrist for some therapy.

However, the first thing she would do today was to visit Chance and work on helping him get through this. She hadn't visited Beth the day before and it was the first time she missed seeing her since her injury. Alex joked to herself that she should get a doctor's note for not visiting Beth.

When Alex started moving around she realized she was sore all over in addition to her face pain. She got dressed slowly and tried to cover as much of the bruise on her cheek as she could with makeup. She usually wore very little makeup but today was an exception, especially since she planned to visit Beth and didn't want her to notice her bruise and ask questions. She called her office before she left and everything was good since Cassie was very capable of running things. Cassie answered, "Alex, are you all right and do you need me to do anything?"

Alex smiled, grateful to her caring staff, especially Cassie. "I am fine and a few days off will work wonders for me. I cannot thank you enough for all of the food and for bringing my car here. How are you holding up?"

Cassie laughed, answering, "I am good but of course I am not the one who got kidnapped, beaten up, and threatened to be killed." Alex laughed hearing what sounded more like the plot of a book and not real life. "Good point but I am going to be fine. Please get me the name of that psychologist we have sent patients to because everyone needs some therapy after a lot of stress like this. It doesn't hurt to be proactive. I will be ready to return to work in a week and thank you again for everything."

It was a warm sunny day which helped to keep Alex's spirits up. Fortunately the hospital was close and she went to see Chance first. She was happy to see him in good spirits even though she was sure his doctor would have visited him to tell him about his injury.

Alex came into his cubicle in the intensive care unit. "How's the patient?"

"Pretty good but I think the metal device suspending my arm is working as an antenna and I am starting to get radio channels. Actually I am good with very little pain." Alex laughed and was happy he still had his sense of humor. Chance continued, "I am bored, restless, getting food that needs work, and the TV channels leave something to be desired. I am afraid that I will start getting into soap operas. Do you think that what happened to you could make a good story line or at least a movie of the week?" Alex laughed at this.

When he told her he was having little discomfort she thought this was a typical male thing from the testosterone making him never admit he was having pain. She did not want to ask how long he would have to be in this contraption because she knew it would be a while and he would have to be hospitalized until there were signs of healing of the bone. Another concern she had was the need for repair of the blood vessels and the possibility of nerve damage. She was pleased that the color of his hand was fairly good which meant he fortunately did have some circulation in his arm. She also knew that he would eventually need more surgery to remove the external splint and to put in a plate for support of the bone. There were compression stockings on his feet to keep him from getting blood clots in his legs and he was to start receiving physical therapy on his other arm and legs to keep the muscles from atrophying. This would be a lengthy recovery and he would not be able to work for a while if at all. She was resolved to keep him cheerful through all of this.

Chance's co- workers were parading through and they brought him real food and things to keep him occupied. His room was filled with flowers, plants and some books to read. The coloring book they brought made him laugh heartily which was a cute diversion. Chance was grateful to them.

After they left she looked at the array of presents and told Chance, "Well it looks like you will have some things to keep you busy although you need your rest. I will be back tomorrow and I will expect a book report when you start reading. You have your cell phone and the hospital phone so you can call any time." They both smiled.

Alex stopped by to see Beth hoping that she wouldn't notice her face and worry. She chuckled when she thought that maybe Beth would laugh at a gift of a coloring book.

On her way home Alex received a phone call from Matthew suggesting that they talk about the evidence that he was given. Alex told him, "I am off this week so tomorrow would be a good time. I am sure you already looked at the diary and the photos and I only have one question."

He was curious and asked, "What is your question?"

Alex answered, "Do you think the diary could win a Pulitzer Prize?" They both laughed which helped relieve

Alex's tension and she now asked seriously, "Am I still in danger?"

Matthew replied, "You shouldn't be unless there are other things in this material you haven't told me about like revealing government secrets or assassination attempts."

This made Alex laugh hard. "What you see is all there is so let me know what time you want to come by and I will make something to eat. I am a pretty good cook."

Matthew commented, "That sounds good and I will call you tomorrow to set up a time."

Alex was relieved to be home. She thought that walking around the pond behind her house and feeding the ducks would take her mind of all of the events that transpired. She knew it would take time but at least all of this was over and she was alright. She worried about the damage to Chance's arm and how much function Chance would get back.

CHAPTER 33

ENDING WITH SAL

Alex went home after checking on Chance at the hospital and she thought about Sal as she did in quiet times.

She heard from Sal often when he was part of her life during her residency which always made her feel good. His schedule was more flexible that hers or he made sure it was, and he started meeting her for lunch or dinner when she was available. She was still a medical resident and had to work long hours including some weekends.

Despite being so busy in her residency, she thought of him often and found herself missing him when they were apart. She often asked herself what she was doing and warning herself to not get involved. Even though she thought of herself as a shameless hussy, she had become very attached to Sal.

She spent a lot of time with Sal on his yacht. The boat was much closer to her work than her place so she often stayed on the ship at night after she was done at the hospital, and even sometimes when he was not there. Her apartment was very modest and far from the hospital because that was all she could afford on her resident's salary.

She was happy with him and that reflected in her demeanor plus her devotion to work. She knew he was married and that this was never going to be anything permanent but fortunately she had her profession which was her future.

Alex never asked for anything from Sal but he showered her with expensive gifts, furs and jewelry insisting that she keep them. He even offered her money and a new car which she declined. Her time on call started becoming less frequent but it did give her more time to spend with him. Alex and had no idea about the generous financial compensation from an unknown source that her fellow residents were receiving for taking over her call. She still had to take some call so that she was not suspicious of what was going on.

Alex was spending a lot of time with Sal she expected that his wife might hire an investigator to look into her husband's activities. Alex never saw anyone suspicious hanging around and the only men she saw were the large muscular ones that were around Sal all the time. Alex and Sal never brought up the subject of love but she could tell how deeply they cared for each other. Never discussing about how they felt made it easier to be together, without stress or expectations. Her diary and photos would remind her for years to come of their special time together.

One morning she woke up on the boat and Sal was already up and about. When she dressed and came out of the cabin, a number of his friends and business associates were having a large meeting over breakfast. She never joined them and Sal never invited her so she went on the back deck enjoying the view where she realized one of his associates Paolo was sitting and smoking a cigar.

He said "Good morning. How well do you know Sal and do you know who he is?"

Alex replied, "We have been friends for a while and we never talk about his business. I guess what Sal wants me to know, he will tell me."

Paolo smiled and commented, "You have spent a lot of time with him and you don't know?"

"I don't understand but know what?" Now her curiosity was sparked.

Paolo laughed, "Have you ever heard of a godfather?"

THE BOXES

Alex replied ignorantly, "Do you mean the person holding a baby when it is baptized?"

Paulo almost could not catch his breath as he started laughing hard. "Sal is the godfather of the largest family organization in this part of the country which is a large syndicate. You really didn't know? Haven't you noticed all of the people coming to see Sal to ask for his help, for favors?"

Alex couldn't answer because so many images flooded into her head. The images of a godfather came to her from the old movies, crime, rubbing people out, and makings people an offer they could not refuse. She felt like a chapter in a book 'dummies who are mistresses' and for being so intelligent, she missed so much. That could have explained the stream of guests on the boat, but she still had trouble believing it.

Alex could not answer right away but mustered, "Thanks for the information but it doesn't matter." She laughed, which was a forced laugh for her, and Paolo went back to the others. Alex never thought of Sal except as a successful businessman and she never suspected that these businesses were of a mafia family. It did not matter because she loved him and nothing changed, except that now she knew that she was the mistress of the married godfather of a very large mafia family. Now she realized why she did not have to worry about any private detectives following her. Who would be stupid enough to follow the girlfriend of a godfather?

Alex was with Sal for over a year and a half, during the rest of her residency and she now felt much better about herself. He restored her feeling of self-worth which was shattered by her severe devastation at the hands of her ex fiancé. She was confident in her ability to practice medicine and she was a skilled surgeon. She knew from the beginning of her relationship with Sal that there was no future with him. She was finishing her residency and felt good but was now ready for a relationship which included marriage and children.

Sal cared deeply for her but understood that the time was coming for her to want a different life. He knew he was selfish keeping the relationship and that it had to end sometime so he enjoyed every minute of it. He felt very lucky to have her in his life even for a little while. She was not like any of his other mistresses, with him for the right reasons and not for material things.

THE BOXES

During the last three months of her residency Alex had been thinking about changing her life. She loved him and enjoyed their time together but it was time to move on. He sensed this when she talked about where her fellow residents were going after they finished.

Two weeks before she finished her residency Alex was sitting with Sal on the upper deck of the boat, holding his hand, looking into his eyes and she finally said, "I am going to start practicing medicine soon and although I care for you, I am ready to get on with my life. I want a family and children which you can't give me." There were tears in her eyes. She felt the pain of longing and regret, afraid to hurt him but this was something she had to do.

He was expecting to hear what she was telling him and sat quietly for a while. This hurt him deeply and he realized how much he was going to miss her. She brought joy to his life and made him happier than he could remember. She was a lovely accomplished woman and he knew she deserved more than what he could give her. He finally said to her, "I knew that our time together would end someday." He tried to smile, hiding his devastation, but he could not change his circumstances.

She looked at him with the tears in her eyes, "This has been very special for me and I was lucky that you found me. You have done more for me than you realize. I will never forget you."

He knew without knowing the details that whatever had happened in her past had a good deal to do with why she even considered being with him. He would never forget her and would miss her every day. They sat quietly for a while not wanting to be separated yet. He finally said, "If there is ever anything that you need or anything I can do to help you, promise me that you will not hesitate to ask," although he knew in his heart that would be unlikely.

She looked into his eyes and replied, "I truly appreciate that but I will be alright. Please don't be angry because I am returning the furs, jewelry, and the other things you gave me. You always knew that they never meant anything to me because I only wanted to be with you. However, I would like to keep the pinky ring you gave me and wearing it will remind me of you." It was a modest ring unlike the lavish jewelry he had given her but she treasured it.

"I know you didn't care but it gave me pleasure to get those things for you." This was more difficult because he knew he had never been this close to anyone except his family but that was a different part of his life. He thought about his other mistresses but he did not keep them around long, and he was nice but did not care much for them. He knew when he and Alex parted that he would never see her again but she would always be in his heart.

They kissed for the last time as she was leaving the boat and Alex had to use every bit of her will power to keep herself from running back into his arms. Sal watched her drive away. She cried all of the way back to her place.

Alex realized she had to find a new life and meet other people. She was a beautiful, educated, intelligent person and the men she had met in the local area wanted to spend time with her until they somehow found out that she was the recently former mistress of a godfather. Moving on was going to be harder than she had anticipated and especially in the area where she was living. She had planned to go someplace where people did not know her or her past so she accepted a job offer in another state, as far away from her life here as she could get. She also changed her name to use her middle name as her last name to make it easier to distance herself from her past and really start over. It would take time to be receptive to having another man in her life but she would, even though she would still never forget Sal.

THE BOXES

The graduation function during which she received the diploma from her residency was a lavish affair but she felt detached and just going through the motions. She mindlessly packed up her few belongings, all of which fit into her car and she left to start her new life. She tried not to think about anything but beginning her practice.

CHAPTER 34

HEALING, THERAPY, END

Chance was a very active person and he was more than ready to leave the hospital after a month. Dr. Franklin removed the external splint on His arm and surgically placed several plates on the bone to stabilize it. The cast they put on was from his shoulder to his hand but fortunately it was only one arm. Pete and Alex visited him every day and were happy to see him progressing while discussing where he would go after the hospital. Alex suggested "You could stay in one of my spare bedrooms upstairs." This pleased Chance but before he could accept her offer, Pete insisted, "You would be much better at my house because I am around more to help out and Alex does have a very busy work schedule. You can stay in your old room." Pete smiled and continued, "Alex and I have already been shopping for convalescing clothing like shirts that open in the front with snaps."

Chance retorted, "Now I feel like a three year old child who is just learning to dress himself." They all laughed.

Chance was in good spirits when Dr Franklin came in. "Your X-rays look good and the cast will keep you out of trouble so how do you feel about getting out of here tomorrow?"

Chance said calmly, "That sounds fine with me." But inwardly he was excitedly jumping up and down at the good news. He knew that he had a long process for healing and rehabilitation. Perhaps it was too soon to ask but he did. "Doc, I know I had a severe injury with a lot of damage to my arm but will I be able to regain full use of it? You know my profession requires me to be able to use firearms."

 Dr. Franklin expected the question and knowing the amount of damage Chance sustained, it was unlikely that Chance could recover completely even though anything was possible. He answered, "We don't know yet and we have to see how you do."

Chance had hoped for a more positive answer but he was willing to do what he could to get better. It was too soon to think about his future.

THE BOXES

Pete smiled when he looked around the room and mentally trying to picture how they could take home all of the gifts brought by friends and work associates. Laughing at his image of three strong men carrying everything out to a large van, he finally turned to Chance and asked him, "Which stuff do you want to take home?" He was hoping that it wasn't a lot.

Thankfully Chance indicated only a few things to leave with and one of them was the coloring book and crayons. This made Alex and Pete laugh heartily.

Chance had been through a great deal and he was beyond being embarrassed by anything. "Hey, it was fun but I got tired of watching soap operas. I don't mind missing what happened in the soap 'As the world ends'." Alex and Pete were laughing so hard at this remark that tears were coming to their eyes.

Chance settled into Pete's house and in a week his large cast was replaced by a smaller one. Alex visited every day and brought food asking, "How is the patient?"

Chance looked forward to her visits, "I am progressing and I am getting better using my left hand although my handwriting looks like that of an uncoordinated first grader." They both chuckled. "Depending on how I am doing the cast may come off in three weeks and then I start physical therapy!"

Alex, "I am happy with your progress." But she still had her concerns about how much function she would have in his arm and hand.

Life was back to normal for Alex. After months of therapy and rehabilitation Chance was be able to use his arm and hand. Alex's psychiatric counseling went well and she was good with no sequelae from her experiences.

Chance could drive now and he met Alex and Pete for lunch at the Italian restaurant where she had first met him. She could tell he wanted to talk. He managed a smile but she could tell how upset he was and he began. "I know my injury was severe and I have undergone a lot of testing to see how much I can do. The nerve damage was substantial and I won't be able to return to my work as a police detective. This job was my life and I don't know what to do now." He was silent and hung his head. Finally, he continued, "I talked to the human resource department and they can put me at a desk job or I have the option of getting disability.

Alex suspected this news but she and Pete were silent. Pete already had a plan.

Pete looked at Chance and began, "You know how busy I have been with my private detective business with too much work for me to do. I have been planning to take in a partner for a while but I need someone with extensive police experience. Are you interested?" He smiled and looked at Chance.

There were tears in all of their eyes when Chance answered, "Yes. Absolutely."

They all hugged and Pete said, "Well now that this is settled so let's eat."

Alex was elated that everything was resolved. Beth was discharged and home with Ben and they were talking about having a family. Chance and Pete were happily going to be working together and now she could devote time to her practice without worries. Sal was gone and even though her memories remained, she was ready to move on with her life.

Alex was very busy with her medical practice but she was now ready to pursue some other interests that she had neglected. While doing some research in her private time when she was a medical student and a resident, she made some discoveries that she wanted to complete. She kept all of the records she had in some boxes that were still at

Beth's house. She was looking forward to working on these.

Reflecting on everything that happened, she felt very lucky that everything turned out well, plus to have incredibly friends, Chance, Beth, Pete and Cassie. Life was good.

THE BOXES

The air was clear with blue skies, and the water was a deep royal blue with only a few ripples from the gentle breeze. Sal was sitting on his expansive balcony overlooking the bay and marina where his one hundred and fifty foot, state of the art yacht was moored. There were lush bushes and an ornate wrought iron fence surrounding the bleached limestone patio. A few steps down was his private pool sparkling from the bright sun. He was drinking a fine Cabernet wine, reflecting on his life and where circumstances had led him.

He had changed his name and his healthy diet and exercise had trimmed his physique to where he wanted it to be, muscled but not too much so. He was a handsome man with thick wavy hair that had some grey, but he looked for younger than his years. A trimmed beard and mustache made him look distinguished and very few of his former associates would recognize him. He was pleased at his choice of relocating to Monaco where life was so different from where he had been. The hotels and casinos that he frequented were brightly lit with ornate decorations but he was always alone.

No one knew he was still alive and he still laughed at the wonderful things said about him in his obituary. He thought it would have been funny for him to attend the memorial service held for him that had been so eloquently described in the newspapers.

Sal often thought about Alex and how much he loved her. He remembered how special their time was when they were together and he regretted never telling her he loved her because of their situation.

There were still some mornings when he was still not fully awake that he expected to find her beside him as it was in the past. To his dismay he realized that she was gone from him to pursue a new life of which he was not a part. The year and a half that they were together was not a long time but he was amazed at how significant an impact she had made on his life. He would never forget her.

Now he had a new life but he did not know how it would progress.

THE BOXES

Sal poured himself another glass of wine and looked fondly at his yacht, which had the name Alexandra scrolled on the back.

www.ingramcontent.com/pod-product-compliance
Lightning Source LLC
Chambersburg PA
CBHW061309170626
46817CB00001B/114